"Do you [...] Miss Franklin?"

Matthew's voice sounded light and pleasant to Jessica.

"No, Mr. Walsingham, we are visiting for a few weeks. My brother's estate is in the North, in County Durham."

It was their turn to lead the set again. When they were once more at rest, she returned the question. "And you, sir. Do you make your home in Bath?"

He gave her an engaging smile. "No, I am staying at the house of my uncle, Lord Stone, in North Parade."

Each innocent enough answer seemed to give them both pause.

"You look monstrous solemn, Miss Franklin. A penny for your thoughts, though I make sure I haven't anything smaller than a crown."

"You are quizzing me, sir. But I promise you my thoughts are not for sale at any price."

" 'Tis just as well, Miss Franklin, for I am much more interested in stealing your heart!"

Books by Carola Dunn

HARLEQUIN REGENCY ROMANCE
25—A SUSCEPTIBLE GENTLEMAN
39—A POOR RELATION
52—A LORD FOR MISS LARKIN

THE FORTUNE-HUNTERS

CAROLA DUNN

Harlequin Books

TORONTO • NEW YORK • LONDON
AMSTERDAM • PARIS • SYDNEY • HAMBURG
STOCKHOLM • ATHENS • TOKYO • MILAN

Published December 1991

ISBN 0-373-31163-X

THE FORTUNE-HUNTERS

CHAPTER ONE

"IT'S NO GOOD," Jessica cried, throwing down her quill in despair. "Even without the outbreak of scabies last autumn and the snowstorm in lambing time, we simply could not make the payment." She had never expected to dread her brother's homecoming. After two years and more fighting in America, Lieutenant Sir Nathan Franklin deserved a joyful welcome, not the shocking news she had to give him. She rose from the small writing desk where she had been studying the figures for the hundredth time and moved restlessly to the window. "When do you think Nathan will arrive, Tibby?"

Miss Tibbett lowered her book and peered over the top of her spectacles at her flaxen-haired former pupil. "It depends on the state of the road from Darlington," she said patiently, not for the first time.

"Some of the fords are bound to be washed out by the snow melt." Jessica gazed out at the steep, greening hills of County Durham. Not a fortnight since they had been blanketed in unseasonable white, at just the wrong moment for the flocks. Now, in the late May sunshine, with puffs of cloud sailing overhead, nothing could have looked more benign.

She pushed aside the faded green velvet curtain to achieve a better view of the carriage drive and there was the long-awaited figure, slim and straight, astride a dapple grey.

"He's here!" Picking up her skirts, she sped from the room, hurried across the hall and flung open the front door just as her brother dismounted. "Nathan! Oh, my dear, you're home at last."

Heedless of the tears of joy streaking down her cheeks, she ran down the steps and hugged him fiercely. He returned the embrace with one arm, the other being occupied with his horse, which snorted in disgust and sidestepped.

"Jess." There was a catch in his throat, too. "It's been so long."

Tad, the indoor man, bounded down the steps to relieve his master of the reins. "I s'll take him round to t'stables, Sir Nathan. Welcome home, sir."

Nathan shook his hand. They were much of an age and had shared more than a few scrapes together in early youth. While they exchanged a word, Jessica stepped back and examined her brother. He had been nineteen when he left Langdale, little more than a boy. At two-and-twenty he was unmistakably a man, tempered in the fire of war. He still bore himself proudly erect as he had ever since he became conscious that his sister had the advantage of him in height as well as age. Though he had grown an inch or two during his absence, he would never be much taller than her, but then she was tall for a female.

She slipped her arm into his. "Come in, Lieutenant Franklin. You must be tired. You are just in time for tea, and Mrs. Ancaster has been baking all your favourites ever since we received your letter from Liverpool."

The butler, Hayes, was waiting at the front door, the folds of his usually lugubrious bloodhound face rearranged in a beam of delight, tears trickling down his wrinkled cheeks. Behind him every servant in the household had already gathered to greet the master, including a stable hand and even one of the shepherds.

Jessica saw that, with his usual punctiliousness, Nathan was going to speak with each of them right down to the scullery maid. Leaving him to it, she rejoined Miss Tibbett in the drawing room.

"How is Sir Nathan?" that lady enquired, going so far as to set her volume aside.

"He looks very well. Handsomer than ever, and his hair still gold to my straw." She tried to pout but laughed for joy. "I cannot bear to spoil today. The bad news can wait until the morning."

With Tibby's support, she succeeded in keeping Nathan busy all evening telling of his adventures in America. Despite the new maturity of his appearance, he had not lost his youthful enthusiasm.

Unfortunately, Jessica thought as she prepared for bed, that probably meant that he was still liable to abrupt descents from the heights to the depths. More than ever she shrank from disclosing the horrid truth. She lay long awake, her mind running round in circles seeking a way out of their difficulties.

Though she was an early riser, Nathan was already at breakfast when she entered the dining room. Miss Tibbett joined them shortly thereafter, just as Nathan said, "Will you ride about the estate with me this morning, Jess? I cannot say how grateful I am for your care of Langdale since Father died."

"I could have done nothing without Rab Mackie," she demurred.

"Yes, I know Father relied on him, and I have no intention of looking for a new factor, I assure you."

The moment could no longer be postponed. Fortifying herself with a gulp of hot, sweet tea, Jessica said, "I fear I have something to tell you which will come as an unpleasant shock."

He frowned and put down his knife and fork. "About Mackie?"

"No, about Langdale. I think we are going to have to leave."

"To leave Langdale? You cannot be serious. The Franklins have been here two hundred years—we leased the land from the Crown even before the Vane family bought Raby Castle."

"One hundred and ninety-eight years come Michaelmas, to be precise. The second ninety-nine year lease is about to expire."

"And Lord Darlington will not renew it?" Nathan sounded puzzled and annoyed, not yet shocked. "Why on earth not? The Vanes have always been most friendly and accommodating. His lordship even helped Father obtain my commission."

"The earl no longer owns Langdale. It has been sold to a Yorkshireman called Scunthwaite. He is asking such an inflated figure for renewal of the lease that I can only suppose he does not want us to take it up. Indeed, we cannot possibly come up with such a sum by Michaelmas, and he refuses to let us take a shorter lease or even to pay in instalments."

Looking at Nathan's suddenly pale face, Jessica wished she had found a way to soften the blow. She put her hand over his but he shook it off.

"There must be something we can do," he said in desperation.

She hesitated.

"Tell him," said Miss Tibbett.

Jessica gazed unseeing at her plate. "Mr. Scunthwaite wants to marry me."

After a moment of heavy silence her brother said tentatively, "I don't suppose..."

"Nathan, he's fifty and *fat!*"

"And shockingly vulgar," Miss Tibbett added.

"I see. Then of course that's out of the question." This time he took her hand. She knew the despair in his hazel eyes was mirrored in her own.

"Marriage!" said Miss Tibbett in a portentous voice. They both turned and stared at her. The long, narrow face bore a look of excitement usually reserved for the acquisition of a new volume of some obscure treatise on Roman Britain. As she nodded meaningfully, her spectacles, perched on top of her head, slid down to entangle themselves in loops of iron grey hair and the ribbons of her plain cambric cap. "That is the answer," she continued, fiddling in an absentminded way with the eyeglasses which now dangled over one ear. "I wonder that I did not think of it sooner."

"But Tibby, you agreed that I cannot possibly marry that dreadful man." As she spoke, Jessica moved around the table to assist in the disentanglement, a task she performed so frequently as to make it automatic.

"There is more than one fish in the sea. Thank you, dear." She returned the spectacles to her nose and peered over them as Jessica resumed her seat. "One of you must find a wealthy spouse."

Sunk in gloom, Nathan did not respond.

"That is all very well," Jessica objected, "but, though I don't mean to boast, most of the eligible gentlemen in the county have been my suitors at one time or another and the few rich ones are already wed."

"County Durham is a desert. We must go to *Aquae Sulis!*"

"To Bath? It's true that the heroines of novels are forever finding husbands there. I suppose there is no other reason for choosing that city?"

Miss Tibbett blushed. "I cannot deny an ulterior motive," she said guiltily. "I have longed this age to see the Roman remains. However, Bath has other advantages. The London Season is almost over, and besides, London is bound to be more expensive."

"And it is easier to gain entrée to Bath Society, I believe." Jessica was beginning to consider the suggestion seriously. "The cost of post horses would be prohibitive, but we could go on the stage, and there must be cheap lodgings to be found."

"Oh dear no, that will never do. If you wish to attract the right sort of person, you must keep up appearances."

"Yes, of course. I shall sell Great-Aunt Matilda's diamonds and we shall do the thing in style."

"No!" Nathan exploded. "I cannot allow you to sell your most valuable jewels for my sake."

"They are too hideously old-fashioned to wear," Jessica pointed out. "Besides, it will be for my sake, too. I have no objection to catching a wealthy husband, just so he be amiable, and even if we fail it will be a famous adventure. You have been all the way to America, but I have never gone farther afield than *Eboracum* and Hadrian's Wall."

"*Eboracum?*" Nathan looked blank. He had spent fewer years under Miss Tibbett's tutelage than his sister.

"The Roman name for York," the governess reminded him.

He made an impatient gesture. "If you are willing to sell the diamonds, Jess, will they not bring enough to pay for the lease?" he asked.

"No, I had already thought of that and had them valued in Durham, but they would pay for a few weeks in Bath and even enable us to cut a dash." Jessica's hazel eyes sparkled at the prospect.

"I cannot countenance such deceit!" cried Nathan. "To put on a show so as to lure innocents into our net would be utterly dishonourable. I had rather resign myself to living in genteel poverty."

"So should not I." The sparkle in her eyes was now militant. "I don't mean to suggest that you should elope with an heiress without her parents' permission. If I am so lucky as to receive an offer from the right sort of gentleman, you may be sure I shall not accept it without revealing my true circumstances. Think of Langdale, Nathan. Can you bear to let it go, after it has been in the family for two centuries, without making every effort to keep it?"

"Of course not," he said wretchedly. "If only there was another way! Surely it would be enough for one of us to marry?"

"To be sure, but if we both make the attempt it will double our chances. You might succeed where I fail. On the other hand, if I am betrothed before you, then you can withdraw from the hunt. The search, I mean," she amended. "Hunt" sounded shockingly mercenary, and her brother's tender sensibilities must be spared.

"I wish I had not sold out," he groaned. "Perhaps I should re-enlist and dash over to Belgium to fight Boney."

"Nathan, no!" Jessica was aghast. "You have done your duty for your country and now it's time to think of yourself and your family."

"Don't worry, Jess, I'm tired of fighting." He managed to smile. "All I want is to settle down and raise sheep. It did not seem too much to hope for."

At last Nathan allowed himself to be persuaded at least to go to Bath. With her usual energy, Jessica at once set about making arrangements. Between Papa's illness, mourning, and Nathan's absence, she had had her fill of responsibilities these past years. It was her duty to her family to try to save Langdale, but she had every intention of enjoying herself in the attempt.

A FORTNIGHT LATER, on a wet evening in mid June, a post-chaise rattled into the yard of the White Hart at Bath. A waiter bearing a huge black umbrella ran up to open the door and Jessica stepped out onto the cobbles, followed by Miss Tibbett, Nathan, and a maid who had been pressed into duty as an abigail. Tad jumped down from the back and the party proceeded into the inn to be greeted by the landlord in person.

"Sir Nathan Franklin?" he said, bowing and rubbing his hands together. "A suite has been reserved as requested, sir. First floor front, overlooking the Pump Room. I trust that will be satisfactory, sir?"

"Most satisfactory," said Miss Tibbett, a gleam in her eye.

"Dinner in half an hour, sir?" enquired the landlord as he ushered them up the stairs.

Nathan remaining moodily silent, Jessica answered, "That will do very well, thank you."

As soon as the door closed behind them, Miss Tibbett rushed to the window of their private parlour. "The

Pump Room!'' she exclaimed rapturously. "Built on the very site where the Romans used to drink the healing waters of Sulis Minerva's sacred well.''

"How did anyone dare commit the sacrilege of building over it?'' Jessica teased, drawing off her gloves as she joined her at the window to peer through the drizzle at the pillared façade opposite. "We shall have a splendid view if it stops raining.''

"I daresay this is the finest room in the house,'' said Nathan in a voice of doom.

"We shall not be here long, for I mean to begin the search for lodgings first thing tomorrow morning. Asking for a garret would have compromised our reputations right from the start.''

"As would arriving by stage coach,'' Miss Tibbett agreed. "It was excessively clever of you, Jessica, to think of hiring a chaise in Chippenham, just for the last stage.''

"And it was clever of Nathan to think of waiting until we reached London to sell the diamonds.'' She saw his expression brighten. "They brought a much better price than the Durham jeweller offered. We shall be able to afford a few extravagances without ruining our budget.''

Tad came in with the luggage and the ladies retired to their chambers to tidy themselves for dinner. Her room was small but comfortable, Jessica noted as she took off her bonnet and set it carefully on the dressing table. It was her best bonnet, the finest Durham had to offer, but she knew it was sadly unmodish. The thought failed to disturb her. She had every intention of refurbishing her wardrobe in the fashionable shops of Milsom Street.

The maid, Sukey, knocked and came in. "Can I help you, miss?'' she offered.

Jessica looked at her, nonplussed. "You could hang up my pelisse," she suggested dubiously.

She had always managed perfectly well without a personal maid, but an abigail was necessary for appearance's sake. Tad was doubtless hovering over Nathan, attempting to play his new rôle of valet, which he was to alternate with that of footman. Jessica smiled as she recalled his delight in his smart bottle-green livery.

For the present, she reminded herself, appearances were all-important.

CHAPTER TWO

"I FEAR MY BROTHER is in something of a miff, Matthew." Miss Caroline Stone regarded her favourite nephew with a worried look as he limped across the maroon-patterned Aubusson to take her hands in his and kiss her cheek.

He smiled down at her, his grey eyes dancing. "If you will go so far as to say Uncle Horace is 'in something of a miff,' I take it he's primed to explode?"

"That might be more accurate," she admitted. "It's no joke, so I wish you will not laugh at me in that odious way. Indeed, my dear, you must tread carefully."

"Don't worry, Aunt Caro, I'll turn the old boy up sweet. That's a mighty becoming cap you have on."

"Flatterer." She touched the froth of Valenciennes lace and coquelicot ribbons perched on her dark hair, streaked with grey though she was not yet forty. "It is pretty, is it not?"

"To be sure, but what I meant is that you are prettier than ever in it. I daresay I had best beard the lion in his den and get it over with. In the library, is he? I rely on you to stitch me up when he is done mauling me—if you will promise not to embroider my hide with rosebuds."

Caroline watched him go, tall, broad-shouldered, jaunty despite his limp, dressed in the pink of fashion. At twenty-seven, he still had the dark hair inherited from her sister without a touch of the early greying which ran in the family. Picking up the embroidery she had been working on when he came down after changing from his travelling clothes, she sighed. Horace had taken some notion into his head and was not going to be easily placated.

Matthew paused in the vestibule for a last check on his appearance. His uncle, Viscount Stone, was a stickler and there was no point setting up the old fellow's back for nothing.

Not without satisfaction, he stared at himself in the looking glass. The swallowtail coat of dark blue superfine, a new one from Scott, fitted without a wrinkle though it was not so tight as to impede his movements. His neckcloth was elegant without ostentation, moderately starched and neatly creased. He gazed thoughtfully at the sapphire pin which nestled in its snowy folds. Would Uncle Horace consider it extravagant? Surely not; the viscount gave him an allowance sufficient to purchase occasional baubles of the kind.

He continued the inventory: modest waistcoat of pale blue satin; skin-tight fawn inexpressibles; boots spotless, glossy yet not so shining as to suggest the expense of champagne in the blacking. While far from being a pinchpenny, Lord Stone regarded wasting money with an attitude not unlike that of a Methodist towards sin.

As he crossed the wide, high Tudor hall, Matthew realized that driving his curricle the ninety miles from London along the busy Bath road had tired him more than he thought. Fatigue always made the wound he had received in the Peninsula ache like the very devil. To limp into his uncle's presence, however, would be too much like a plea for sympathy.

Knocking on the library door, he entered the book-lined room and strode with steady steps towards the small, white-haired man behind the large mahogany desk.

"How are you, Uncle?" he asked cheerfully.

"None the better for the news I had t'other day from half a dozen busybodies in Town," snorted Lord Stone, scowling. "Don't stand there towering over me, Walsingham. I can't abide it."

Matthew was glad to pull up a chair, but his uncle's unusual use of his surname worried him. "I came as fast as I could on receiving your letter."

"Wearing out that high-stepping pair o' bays you're so proud of, I daresay."

"No, sir, I left them at the first stage with Hanson to bring them on slowly."

"And wasted the blunt on hired horses! You might as well have told him to take them back to Town, for you'll not be staying here long. I've had enough of your care-for-nobody ways. Pushing your chère-amie in a wheel-barrow down St. James's Street in her petticoats! Disgraceful!"

Matthew tried to repress a grin at the memory of Lulu kicking up her heels and squealing with delight. "It was a race, sir, for a wager."

"Aye, so I've heard. Two hundred guineas!"

"But, Uncle, I . . ."

"Two hundred guineas!" the viscount repeated, purpling at the thought. "Your trouble, my boy, is that you have no comprehension of the value of money. You'll learn it soon enough when you have to manage on the pittance your father left you. My lawyer's coming tomorrow to change my will in favour of your cousin Archibald. Not another penny will you get from me." A thump of fist on desk punctuated this declaration.

Matthew was aghast. To lose his income now and Stone Gables in the future, all for a harmless prank that, in a more sanguine humour, the viscount would have laughed at as a very good joke. And to lose it to his sanctimonious cousin Archibald Biggin—it didn't bear thinking of. Yet the lawyer was already sent for. Once Lord Stone had made up his mind, argument only hardened his determination, and Matthew was not prepared to crawl, not even in such dire straits.

All the same, there were others to be thought of.

"I have debts in London, sir," he said tentatively.

"Gaming debts, no doubt," his uncle growled. "You need not think I shall pay them. From now on you'll not be moving in fashionable circles anyway, so what matter if you are cast out of decent society."

"Not gaming debts, sir. It was you who taught me to play and pay."

"A little genteel betting on the cards for modest stakes, not two hundred guineas for a scandalous jape! You owe your tradesmen, I suppose."

"Yes, sir."

"Doubtless they are used to whistling for their money. It's just as well you told your groom to come on here, for you'll not be daring to show your face in Town. I suppose you'll have to stay until he arrives. Now get out, and tell Caroline I'll dine on a tray in here."

Matthew stood up and leaned with both hands on the desk. His leg ached fiercely. "I suppose it's no good promising to reform," he said.

"Too late. I've been patient with you and this is the last straw. Now get out! Get out!" shouted the viscount.

The march back down the long room seemed endless. Matthew closed the door softly behind him and slumped against it. Then he realized the butler was lurking nearby. Straightening, he attempted a smile.

"I'm afraid his lordship's in a devil of a passion, Bristow."

"He's been cross as a bear with a sore head all week, Mr. Matthew. It's the collywobbles—dyspepsia the sawbones calls it. Well, you know for yourself, sir, how his lordship likes his food."

"Too much jugged hare, eh? Mrs. Bristow's cooking is enough to tempt any man to overindulge. My uncle asked for a tray in the library this evening."

He returned to the drawing room, but Aunt Caroline had gone up to change for dinner so he had to wait until they met, at one end of the long dining table, to pour out his woes.

"I shan't starve, of course," he said gloomily, helping himself to a second serving of vegetable marrow stuffed with minced veal. "The Consols my father left me bring in around four hundred and fifty a year. But I shall have to choose whether to live by my wits on the fringes of Society or to abjure the Polite World altogether."

"You might consider taking up a respectable profession," his aunt proposed.

Matthew brightened. "I have always been interested in architecture, though I consider it merely a hobby. The trouble is it would take a long time to get started, and I have debts that ought to be paid soon: my tailor, my bootmaker, my landlady, the coal merchant, and at least half a dozen others. You don't suppose Uncle Horace will relent?''

"I wish I could give you some hope, but Horace has always refused to listen to persuasion, since he was a small boy, according to your mama. I recall her telling me of an occasion when she was eight—he would have been six—when he insisted on going shoeless in the snow. No matter what anyone said, only the actual experience of frozen toes changed his mind.''

"I shall have no opportunity of proving myself sober and frugal, since he will doubtless consider that in my straitened circumstances I have no choice.'' He sighed. "You know, Aunt Caro, it's dashed rotten timing.''

"Very true, alas. If he had not heard from those busybodies at a time when he is suffering from dyspepsia, I daresay he would have thought your antics a very good joke.''

"Yes, there's that, but what I meant is that I'd just about had enough of cutting up larks anyway. It's not as if I meant to spend the rest of my life on the spree.''

She patted his arm. "I have often thought that your enthusiastic embrace of the amusements of Town was more of an attempt to forget the horrors of war than a defect of character.''

He lifted her hand to his lips and kissed it. Half his friends dead in the Peninsula and himself laid up for the better part of a year, not knowing if he would ever walk again—yes, the horrors of war was one way to describe it. "Dearest Aunt, you may just be right.'' His smile was crooked. "However, it's past time to put the wretched business behind me. I shall strive to become a useful citizen.''

"That seems to be your best course," she said, laughing at his dismal tone, "unless you can find an heiress to marry."

His fork half way to his mouth, he stopped with an arrested look. "Now there is a famous notion. It will take some time to set up as an architect, so I might as well look about me for a rich bride in the meantime."

"Why not? Bath was said to be a fertile ground for fortune hunters in my youth. The living was cheaper and the competition less than in London."

She was teasing, but the more Matthew thought about it the more it seemed an excellent solution. At worst, Bath would provide superb buildings for him to study in pursuit of his new profession.

"And it's only fifteen miles," he said, "so I shan't spend a penny on post horses getting there."

"You really mean to do it?"

"Don't look so worried, Aunt. I've no intention of abducting my heiress should I be so lucky as to find one. All fair and square and above board." Well, nearly, he admitted to himself. If he was perfectly honest about his comparative poverty he would never meet an heiress in the first place. He'd have to put up a show. "I don't suppose it would be possible to stay at Uncle Horace's house on North Parade?"

"He never goes there," she said doubtfully, "since he blames the waters for ruining his digestion. Certainly they always made him bilious. He has really only kept the house because when there are no tenants I like to spend a few days there occasionally. In fact he was talking of selling it, and it is not let at present, I believe."

"Be a dear and give me a letter to the housekeeper," he coaxed. "Is it still the same woman?"

"Yes. She always had a soft spot for you and never fails to ask after you. Very well, Matthew, I shall aid and abet you in this horrid scheme, and we must hope that my brother never comes to hear of it."

"On the contrary. I cannot think of anything more like to persuade him of my respect for money than to turn up with a wealthy wife on my arm."

"Possibly." She shook her head wryly. "I can let you have twenty pounds to keep the wolf from the door for the present."

"Bless you, but if I am to save the cost of lodgings by staying in North Parade, I can manage until quarter day. That's what is so infuriating about the whole business," he added with a rueful grin. "Uncle Horace is on his high ropes because of that wager—and I won it!"

CHAPTER THREE

THE FIRST THING Jessica did on their first morning in Bath was to send Nathan to obtain subscriptions to the Pump Room, the Assembly Rooms, both Upper and Lower, and Harrison's Circulating Library and Reading Room. She would not for the world have him go with her to hire lodgings, or they would find themselves tucked away up a pair of back stairs in a back street.

Having obtained from the landlord the name and direction of a reputable house agent, she and Miss Tibbett set off for Old Bond Street. The pale amber Bath stone of which so much of the town was built seemed to catch and reinforce the sunlight, a pleasant change after yesterday's dreary weather. Jessica kept her hand firmly tucked under her companion's arm, for Tibby kept casting longing looks towards the Pump Room as they passed. Indeed, so determined was she on looking backwards that they had a narrow escape from the wheels of a phaeton as they crossed the busy corner of Cheap Street.

"You shall explore the baths to your heart's content as soon as we are settled in lodgings," Jessica promised, "if you manage to survive until then."

She herself found it difficult to resist the lure of the shop windows, but they reached their destination without further mishap. The house agent assured them that they had arrived early enough in the Bath Season to have a wide choice of desirable residences in all areas of the town.

"The upper part is considered more salubrious," he explained, "and is therefore more expensive."

"Expense is no object," said Jessica with a dismissive wave of the hand. "However, my aunt wishes to reside within easy walking distance of the baths, so we will stay in the lower part of town, if you please." An aunt, she felt, was a more impressive chaperone than a former governess.

"I'm sorry to hear madam is indisposed," he said, hopefully inquisitive. Jessica was sure that any information she provided was bound to reach a wide audience.

"I am not in the least indisposed," snapped Miss Tibbett, absorbing without a quiver her unexpected promotion. "I wish to explore the remains of *Aquae Sulis*."

"Ak...? Oh, the Roman ruins. Let me see what I can do for you, madam." He ran his finger down a list. "There's a nice place in Pulteney Street. It's a bit of a walk, but level all the way. Then there's North Parade, that's closer, only it's the end house, right by the river. There's a lot of people don't care for the river's miasmas, so it's going a bit cheaper."

Jessica clasped her hands in well-feigned delight. "By the river? How charming! You don't fear the miasmas, do you, Aunt Tibby?"

"Not in the least. You know I am not at all invalidish." She glared at the unforgiven agent. "I find the sound of running water an excellent soporific."

"And I adore sketching rivers. We shall take it."

"I think you'll be pleased, Miss Franklin. You can see Pulteney Bridge from the upper windows. Will you be requiring servants? I can engage them for you."

"Thank you, but I prefer my own staff," said Jessica grandly. "They will arrive tomorrow from my brother's estate in the North." She hoped he pictured a large carriage bearing at least a dozen servants, not Hayes and Mrs. Ancaster hopping off the stage.

"Of course there is a housekeeper comes with the house."

"Oh no, that will never do!" Aghast, she foresaw the woman gossiping about the footman who turned into a valet, and the housemaid playing the abigail.

Miss Tibbett came to the rescue. "The truth is, Sir Nathan cannot abide strange servants about him."

"Well, I daresay she will be glad of a holiday," he said doubtfully.

"My brother is recently returned from America and he—ah—he prefers to surround himself with familiar faces now that he is home," Jessica improvised. The man accepted her explanation with a nod of sympathetic comprehension. Doubtless he thought Nathan's nerves had suffered in the war. Nathan would be furious if he ever found out. "Of course we have not cared for amusements during his absence," she hurried on. "Since estates are so large in the North, Langdale is rather isolated and I fear we are fallen behind the mode. Perhaps you could advise us as to which shops are the most fashionable?"

Armed with this information and the key to Number 15, North Parade, Jessica and Aunt Tibby picked up Nathan at the White Hart and went to inspect their new home.

As they crossed Pierrepont Street and started down North Parade, a smart curricle came towards them. Deep blue with yellow-painted trim, it was pulled by a pair of bays which drew a whistle of admiration from Nathan. His attention attracted by the sound, the driver grinned and saluted with his whip. Nathan turned to stare after the vehicle. Tugging on his arm, Jessica glanced back and found the gentleman doing likewise. She blushed in confusion, torn between wishing she had already purchased a new bonnet and hoping that he didn't think she was so bold as to deliberately catch his eye.

"What a splendid rig," said Nathan enviously. "I'll wager that set him back a pretty penny."

"He must be wealthy then." Jessica could not resist another backward glance but the curricle was gone. "I wonder if he's married. He appeared to be quite young."

Reminded of their purpose in coming to Bath, Nathan was once more cast into the dismals. He merely grunted when his sister demanded his opinion of Number 15.

"Well, I think it's quite perfect," she said. "Not too large, elegantly furnished, close to the centre of town." And possibly in the same street as the rich gentleman with the boyish grin, she added to herself. "We shall move in tomorrow."

By the following evening they were settled in North Parade. Tad, in his livery, was sent to meet the stage and brought Hayes and Mrs. Ancaster to join them. Satisfied with her arrangements, Jessica retired to her chamber, prepared for bed, and snuffed her candle. She went to sit at the window, gazing out at the Avon. In the last light of sunset, the water frothed pink as it rushed over the weir below Pulteney Bridge. Above the three dark arches, lamps still burned in the windows of the little shops that lined the bridge.

Gradually Jessica's gaze turned to the gardens opposite the house, deserted at this late hour, and then to the street leading towards the town centre. The lamplighter was making his rounds. A carriage rumbled past him and stopped outside the building next to theirs, but in the dusk, at an awkward angle, she could not make out whether it was a curricle, let alone who the driver was.

It was ridiculous the way her thoughts kept turning to the gentleman of whom she had caught no more than a glimpse, she scolded herself. Probably she would never see him again, and if she did she might very well not recognize him. And if he should by chance recognize her, doubtless he would recall her as the brazen hussy who had stared at him in the street.

She laughed, shook her head, and went to bed. As Tibby said, there were plenty of fish in the sea. Seeking the right one was going to be an adventure and, much as she loved Langdale, how she had longed for adventure these past years.

LOOKING AROUND the Pump Room the next morning, Jessica wondered if Tibby's maxim was true. Crutches, ear trumpets, and Bath chairs abounded. Except for herself and Nathan, as far as she could see, Miss Tibbett was the youngest person there by a decade.

"Dash it, they're all octogenarian invalids," Nathan exclaimed indignantly. "You need not think I shall marry a female old enough to be my grandmother, however rich."

"Hush! Of course not," Jessica whispered. "I believe we may have come too early, before the fashionable hour, but it was impossible to make Aunt Tibby wait any longer."

Miss Tibbett also was gazing about her, but her displeasure was reserved for the building. "Nothing here older than a hundred years," she said in disgust.

"And no *one* much younger," said Jessica, laughing despite her dismay. "Perhaps it is just as well, as we have not yet visited the modiste. Since we are here, you must drink a glass of water, Aunt. That, surely, has not changed since Roman days."

This suggestion finding favour, Miss Tibbett made her way across the room to the pump. Nathan and Jessica strolled to the end where, in an alcove, stood a statue of Beau Nash, a stout, bewigged gentleman in a frock coat. Only the bottom three buttons of his thigh-length waistcoat met over his bulging stone stomach.

"I'm dashed if I can see how he ever earned the nickname 'Beau'," said Nathan.

"Bath was a much more fashionable resort when he ruled here," Jessica mourned. "I hope we are not come on a wild goose chase."

They turned to look back down the vista of decrepitude, brightly illumined by huge windows between Corinthian columns. Of Miss Tibbett's neat, spare figure, clad in her habitual black, there was no sign.

"The lady asked the way to the baths," said the pump attendant when they enquired. "If you go out through that door there, likely you'll find her."

The sulphurously steaming baths they found. Miss Tibbett had vanished.

"No doubt she's investigating the foundations by now," Nathan guessed.

"Never mind. The house is not much more than a furlong from here so she cannot possibly lose her way home. *Dearest* brother, will you go with me to the shops?"

Indulgently, Nathan agreed. Whatever he thought of her totty-headed plan, Jessica deserved a new wardrobe and a few weeks of frivolity. She had kept Langdale going for him during his absence with never a murmur of complaint. How she spent the money from the sale of her diamond heirloom was her affair, after all, and it was not fair to spoil her pleasure by moping.

He had no intention of compromising his honour by becoming a fortune hunter, so what harm could there be in enjoying the entertainments of Bath?

"Are we to attend the ball at the Upper Rooms tomorrow night?" he enquired, offering his arm as they crossed the Pump Yard, passed under the colonnade and turned right in Stall Street.

"If I can find a seamstress who will make me a gown in time. How lucky it is that modern fashions are so simple. In Beau Nash's day, with all the silks and brocades and hoops they wore, it must have taken weeks to produce a single garment. I shall look for a white muslin sprigged in the green of the tunic I have been netting, and I should like a wreath of white roses with green leaves for my hair."

"I shall have the pleasure of escorting the most beautiful and elegant female in the place," he said gallantly. Indeed he was proud to parade her on his arm, and he noted more than one admiring glance cast in her direction despite her unmodish dress.

The streets were busy now, and he was glad to see that a reasonable proportion of the inhabitants of the town appeared to be under forty years of age. A trio of young ladies tripped down Old Bond Street towards them, twirling parasols of pink and blue and primrose yellow. As they passed they cast sidelong looks at him, and whispered and giggled.

Suddenly he was conscious of his own shabby, provincial appearance. He had arrived home from America with nothing but his uniform, and apart from a cheap coat bought in Liverpool, his entire wardrobe was three years old or more. Fortunately, as a boy he had worn his clothes loose-fitting, being more interested in country sports than dandyism. Nonetheless, the sleeves of his coat were a good inch too short, and only the knit fabric and the stirrup-straps of his pantaloons allowed them to stretch to a fashionably skintight fit.

"If you don't mind," he said, avoiding his sister's eye, "I shall escort you to the draper's shop and abandon you there while I find a tailor."

Laughter quivered behind the solemnity of her tone as she replied, "By all means. If I am not at the draper's when you come to find me, try the milliner's next door."

Let her suppose that he was falling in with her nefarious stratagems! Because he chose to be decently dressed did not mean he intended to worm his way into the affections of some innocent heiress.

THE NEXT EVENING, as Jessica stepped down from her sedan chair outside the Assembly Rooms, she acknowledged being pleased with herself. She had asked the draper for the name of a seamstress who might be able to make up a gown at short notice. He had supplied a name and direction. The woman was not, he said deprecatingly, a fashionable modiste, but for that reason she was not likely to be busy.

The seamstress, a widow in reduced circumstances, had been touchingly grateful for the work. She was quick and competent, her charges were moderate, and Jessica had every intention of continuing to patronize her.

The new sprigged muslin gown was all she had hoped, with the net tunic adding a touch of elegance. She had even found green kid dancing slippers to match. Her pale hair was pinned in a topknot wreathed by silk daisies, with a few curls on her forehead and artful tendrils escaping to caress her neck. In the slanting evening sunlight, Mama's aquamarines sparkled as brightly as emeralds.

Nathan, paying off the chairmen, was bang up to the mark in a glossy new beaver, forest-green coat of Bath superfine, dove-coloured inexpressibles, green satin waistcoat, and cravat tied in a Waterfall over which she knew he and Tad had struggled for a good forty-five minutes. He was even wearing Papa's heavy gold signet ring, and from his fob dangled a miniature gold monkey with ruby eyes that a seafaring uncle had brought him from India when they were children. Just enough to hint at wealth without being ostentatious, she thought with an approving nod, though she doubted that Nathan saw it that way.

Now he was handing Miss Tibbett down from her chair. In her best black silk, "Aunt" Tibby was the patterncard of a thoroughly respectable chaperone. She wore the string of oval jet beads separated by tiny gold balls that Jessica had purchased for her that afternoon at Perrin's, the best jeweller in Milsom Street. The necklace, together with her air of suppressed excitement, made her look less like a governess than ever. She had even consented to leave her spectacles at home.

Miss Tibbett had found a Roman coin that morning and she was eager to share the news with anyone she could persuade to listen.

The Master of Ceremonies, Mr. Guynette, bowed graciously when Nathan announced their names and wished them a pleasant stay in Bath. They moved on into the ballroom and found seats on the benches at the side.

At the end, beneath a statue of a female figure in Classical draperies bearing a lyre, the orchestra tuned up as the room filled. Watching the flow of new arrivals, Jessica remained satisfied with her and her companions' appearance. Less satisfactory was the realization that everyone seemed to know everyone else, or at least a few others, while she and Nathan had not a single acquaintance among the crowd. She longed to be able to jump up with a cry of delight and greet some "dearest friend," as every other young lady seemed able to do.

How futile it was to know she was looking her best if no one noticed!

Couples began to take their places on the floor. Jessica was about to urge Nathan to go and ask Mr. Guynette to present him to some partnerless female when that gentleman bustled up with a short, plump, red-cheeked young man in tow.

"Miss Franklin," he said, beaming, "Mr. Barlow has particularly requested an introduction. I trust you will regard him with favour as a partner in the country dance. Sir Nathan, you are not yet standing up. Come with me, pray, and I shall find you a pretty miss."

As he bore Nathan away, Jessica rose to find herself, as she had feared, an inch or two taller than Mr. Barlow. However, it was unthinkable to refuse the Master of Ceremonies' command, even if she could have brought herself to disappoint the young gentleman gazing at her hopefully.

"It's fate," he announced in a mournful voice as he led her to the nearest incomplete set. "I cannot help myself. I always fall in love with tall females."

She laughed and made up her mind to enjoy herself.

Mr. Barlow, eldest son of a West-Country squire, proved to be an amusing rattle, and the next gentleman presented by Mr. Guynette made up for his lack of inches. Lord Peter Something-she-didn't-catch was excessively tall and painfully thin, with a haughty nose which suggested generations of aristocratic forebears. Trying to talk to him while standing beside him, she developed a crick in the neck. Her effort was wasted, too, for he had absolutely no conversation and responded to her openings with grunted monosyllables. Nor did he appear to have much acquaintance with the steps of the country dance. She consoled herself with the thought that he was a younger son, and therefore a poor prospect.

Returning to Aunt Tibby after the set, she was determined to sit out the next dance. Her resolution vanished like summer dew when Mr. Guynette reappeared with the gentleman of the curricle at his side.

CHAPTER FOUR

"MR. WALSINGHAM, ma'am," announced the Master of Ceremonies before trotting off about his kindly duties.

Jessica looked up into admiring grey eyes set in a face somewhat too long to be called handsome but with an attractively humorous cast. He was rather taller than she had expected from her brief view, well-built though lean. The fit of his black coat over his broad shoulders betokened a first class tailor, while the sapphire pin adorning his simply tied cravat suggested affluence with no aspirations to dandyism.

He gave no sign of having recognized her.

He bowed, and she noted with approval the crisp curl of his short, dark hair. "May I have the pleasure of this dance, Miss Franklin?" His voice was a light, pleasant tenor.

Rising, she returned his smile and curtsied. "Thank you, sir, that will be delightful."

As they walked out onto the floor she saw that he limped slightly. There had to be a flaw, she thought philosophically. No one could possibly be quite as perfect as Mr. Walsingham had at first appeared.

"Do you live in Bath, ma'am?" he enquired politely as they waited for the music to start up.

"No, sir, we are visiting for a few weeks. My brother's estate is in the North, in County Durham."

"After so long a journey I trust you are enjoying your stay in Bath?"

"Oh, yes," she said with conviction. The beginning of a dance prevented her elaborating on this brief answer for a few minutes. He danced well, performing the figures with aplomb, his limp scarcely in evidence.

Then it was the next couple's turn to take up the steps and Jessica continued, "We had thought of going to London but I abhor crowds. I confess, though, that I was not sure, yesterday morning, whether we had made a mistake in coming here. We arrived at the Pump Room before the fashionable hour." She described the company in which they had found themselves, and Nathan's horror. "So you see, we were vastly gratified to find this evening that we are not the only people here with the full use of our limbs. Oh!" She raised her hand to her mouth with a horrified gasp, feeling her cheeks turn scarlet. "I beg your pardon, sir!"

To her relief, it was time to curtsy to her neighbour and turn on his arm. She avoided Mr. Walsingham's eye as they exchanged places with the couple opposite. How could she have said such a thing! She would not blame him if he cut her dead in future, though he was too gentlemanly to abandon her on the dance floor.

"A war wound, Miss Franklin," he said gravely, but there was something in his voice that gave her courage to risk an upward peek. To her great indignation, his eyes were laughing at her. "I was invalided out of the army," he explained.

"You were in the Peninsula with Wellington?" she ventured. "My brother has just returned from America. He will be pleased to meet another soldier, if you will forgive my ill-considered remark and allow me to introduce you."

"Consider it unsaid. May I hope that you will acknowledge the acquaintance when next you meet me in the Pump Room in my Bath chair?"

"I shall offer to push you for a turn about the room, and bully you into drinking up your glass of spring water."

"So fair a face yet so unkind," he said with mock outrage. "Have you tasted the stuff?"

"It smelled so horrid I could not bring myself to try it. You are not here to take the waters, I trust."

"N... Yes, alas. I refuse to boil myself in the baths like a lobster, but the doctors think that drinking a daily draught may be of value for...er...for my chest. A minor wound to the lung." He coughed hollowly, provoking astonished stares from their fellow dancers.

It was their turn to lead the set again. Jessica was glad that the exertion of dancing did not seem to have an ill effect on Mr. Walsingham's injured lung, since his alarming cough did not recur. When they were once more at rest, she asked, "You do not live in Bath, then?"

"No, I am staying at the house of my uncle, Lord Stone, in North Parade."

This innocent answer was pronounced in a significant tone that at once made her suspect that he did indeed remember her after all. If he already thought her a disgracefully forward female, that would explain why he had not taken offence at her unfortunate comment. Doubtless he considered her incapable of ladylike reticence.

"You look monstrous solemn, Miss Franklin. A penny for your thoughts."

"They are not worth a farthing, sir," she assured him hastily.

He felt in his pockets. "I fear I have no farthing, nor a penny. Nothing smaller than a crown, and I feel sure you are too honest to accept a crown for what is not worth a farthing."

"You are quizzing me, sir, but I promise you I should not tell you my thoughts even if you did happen to have a farthing in your pocket."

"I'm glad to hear it, ma'am. In that case I can tease you on the matter whenever we meet, and we shall never lack for a subject of conversation."

Jessica laughed, but as she completed the final figure of the dance she was aware of a warm glow of content. It sounded very much as if the amiable Mr. Walsingham wanted to see her again.

When he escorted her back to the benches, she discovered that her spurious aunt was missing. Dismayed, she scanned the room. Miss Tibbett was nowhere to be seen. Propriety frowned on a young lady sitting alone, yet she hesitated to ask Mr. Walsingham to stay, or to help her search for her chaperone. He might—horrid thought!—suppose that she had deliberately arranged with Aunt Tibby to disappear.

She was glad to see her brother approaching. "Nathan, have you seen our aunt?"

"Don't tell me she has mislaid herself again," he said, grinning. "I doubt there are Roman ruins in this part of town."

"Roman ruins?" Mr. Walsingham enquired in surprise.

Jessica introduced the gentlemen to each other and explained about Miss Tibbett's ruling passion. "I only hope she is not wandering outside in the dark hunting for sesterces," she sighed. "It's all very well vanishing from the Pump Room in broad daylight, but to abandon me in a ballroom at night is the outside of enough."

"I'll take care of you, Jess," Nathan assured her. "I was coming to look for you anyway. It's time for tea and I have left my last partner and her mama waiting for us in the tea room. I daresay Aunt Tibby is in there, too. Sir, will you join us if you are not engaged elsewhere?"

Mr. Walsingham accepted with flattering alacrity and they proceeded to the tea room. Nathan's partner turned out to be Mr. Barlow's sister, a lively girl as short and round-cheeked as her brother, who also made one of the party. He welcomed Jessica with every evidence of delight, proclaiming himself an old friend.

Nathan and Mr. Walsingham fell into a discussion of the Peninsula and American Wars. Happy to see them on cordial terms, Jessica allowed herself to be monopolized by the Barlows. Mrs. Barlow, a matronly version of her offspring, chatted placidly about the amusements of Bath while she poured the tea. Her daughter was a friendly young lady who very soon begged Jessica to call her Kitty.

"When I am addressed as Miss Barlow," she explained with a giggle, "I look around for my sister Amelia, though she has been married for several years now. Mama has brought us all in turn to Bath when we turned eighteen, and my sisters have all made very respectable matches."

Mrs. Barlow nodded complacently. "I fancy I can congratulate myself, Miss Franklin, for it is no joke, you know, to have five daughters to turn off."

"It'll be no trouble to dispose of Kitty," said Mr. Barlow, "for she's the best natured of my sisters and a taking little thing. Why, I'd marry her myself in an instant if she only had a fortune.''

This witticism provoked a merry laugh from Kitty. Jessica smiled, deciding that she liked the cheerful family. Despite the five years between herself and Miss Barlow, it would be agreeable to have a female friend with whom to shop and walk, someone to look out for at entertainments when Tibby disappeared.

Tibby! Where had she got to? Jessica cast a glance about the room, but the waiters scurrying between the tables and latecomers looking for seats hid half the company from view.

"Mr. Barlow, have you by any chance seen my aunt?''

"'Fraid I don't recall the lady, ma'am. From the moment I first set eyes on your face, dashed if I could tear 'em away long enough to note anyone else's.''

Miss Tibbett continued least in sight. However, under Mrs. Barlow's kindly aegis, Jessica stood up with three more gentlemen presented by Mr. Guynette, and had the doubtful felicity of finding herself in the same set as Mr. Walsingham and his partner of the moment.

Though he treated the young lady with a grave courtesy quite unlike his teasing way with Jessica, she scarcely raised her eyes beyond his middle waistcoat button. Possibly because of the weight of her diamond aigrette, thought Jessica with unusual waspishness. The spray of jewels in her hair was part of a parure consisting of a collar, ear-bobs, brooch, and bracelets, fit for a duchess to wear to St. James's Palace. It was amazing that the glittering creature could dance at all.

Her gown was buttercup-yellow satin with an overdress of what Jessica suspected was genuine Valenciennes lace. Amidst the pastel muslins she looked like a peacock among doves. Yet she appeared to be bashful to the point of timidity.

Turning on Mr. Walsingham's arm, Jessica caught his half laughing, half exasperated glance and was somewhat consoled.

The ball ended promptly at the early hour of eleven, in accordance with Beau Nash's dictum, which had survived its originator by half a century. When Jessica and Nathan followed the dispersing crowd into the anteroom, Miss Tibbett was waiting there for them.

"Aunt Tibby, you look smug as the cat that stole the cream. What have you been up to?" Jessica demanded.

"I have made the acquaintance of a charming couple," she explained. "A retired clergyman and his wife, and—" she took a deep breath, her eyes sparkling with delight "—they are both amateur archaeologists with a particular interest in Roman Bath!"

Jessica hadn't the heart to take her to task for abandoning her charge in the ballroom.

Every chairman in Bath was waiting at the doors of the Assembly Rooms, so they soon reached home. Exhausted by the excitement, Tibby retired at once. All the servants had gone to bed long since, but Jessica and Nathan repaired to the kitchen to discuss the events of the evening.

Jessica poked up the fire and heated milk for hot chocolate while Nathan ransacked the pantry for edibles.

"Do you mean to set your cap at Walsingham?" He reappeared with a plateful of strawberry tartlets in one hand and the remains of one of the sticky pastries in the other. "I cannot like the thought of deceiving him. He's a famous fellow."

"Would you prefer that I set my cap at a rogue? Not that I mean to 'set my cap' at anyone, but I like Mr. Walsingham very well."

"Only think, I happened to mention how much I admired his curricle and his cattle, and he offered to take me up in it, and even to let me handle the ribbons!"

"Oh, Nathan, you didn't remind him that we saw him driving down this very street!"

"Why the devil should I not?" he asked in surprise. "But no, I don't believe I said where I had seen him. He was surprised that we had no vehicle with us, so I told him your taradiddle about having heard the Bath streets were too steep for carriages and it's easier to take a chair."

"It's no taradiddle," Jessica said indignantly. "I know I read that somewhere."

"Never mind. I also said that I intend to purchase a curricle but I have had no opportunity since returning from America, which is perfectly true. And Walsingham offered to give me his advice..."

"You haven't committed yourself to buying a curricle!"

"I wish you will not interrupt a fellow so, Jess. As I was about to say, his first word of advice was not to buy in Bath because the best carriage-builders are in London. So you see, you need not put yourself in a tweak. I know perfectly well we cannot afford any such extravagance. You ought to be grateful to me for upholding your bluff, for I *cannot* approve of it."

"I'm sorry, my dear, and I am grateful, I promise you. Did you at least enjoy the ball?"

"Yes," he admitted with a wry smile. "I met a number of good fellows and danced with several delightful girls. I've no desire to marry any of them, however, and I cannot even tell you whether any of them are rich!"

CHAPTER FIVE

MATTHEW WHISTLED as he strolled towards the Pump Room. The world was a bright place this fine June morning. Not ten minutes ago he had seen, from his uncle's conveniently placed dining room window, Miss Franklin setting out in this direction with her aunt at her side. At this hour the chances were better than even that the Pump Room was their destination.

He could not believe his luck. Within two days of his arrival in Bath he had met a handsome, agreeable young lady whose brother owned vast estates in the North. What was more, she seemed to like him, and Sir Nathan was a pleasant enough young cub who was unlikely to stand in his way. Jess, he had called her. Jessica? Jessamine? Pretty names, both. Either would suit her to a T.

How she had blushed when he had hinted at recalling her backward glance in North Parade! Of course he knew perfectly well that she had been looking at her brother, not at him, but he had every intention of continuing to tease her about it. She was not sure yet whether he had recognized her—as if he could have mistaken or forgotten that glorious ash-blond hair! Yes, she had been enchantingly abashed, yet in general she was a spirited young lady.

In that she differed from Miss Pearson. He had struggled to draw a response from Miss Pearson, and

her rare replies to his remarks were spoken so softly he
had not the least notion what she had said. She had
worn a dazzling fortune in diamonds upon her person,
but to his mind Miss Franklin's sparkling hazel eyes
were more attractive by far.

He turned the corner of the Abbey and there before
him stood the subject of his musing, fresh and pretty in
apricot muslin with white ribbons, a saucy leghorn hat,
and a frilly white parasol. She was alone, gazing up in
apparent fascination at the west front of the church.

It was not strictly correct to accost a young lady in the
street unless she first acknowledged one's presence, but
he'd be damned if he'd pass by without a word. "Good
morning, Miss Franklin."

Starting, she turned to him with a smile. "Good day,
Mr. Walsingham. Have you ever noticed the angels
climbing the ladder up the tower?"

"A charming conceit, is it not? It's said to commem-
orate the vision which inspired the building of the Abbey—a bishop called Oliver King who dreamt about a
crowned olive tree and angels on a ladder and somehow interpreted it as a command to rebuild the place."

"There's no accounting for visions," Jessica agreed.
"I must bring my sketch book here one day. Bath is full
of pleasant prospects."

"It is, indeed," he agreed, regarding her slim figure
with appreciation. "Are you on your way to the Pump
Room?"

"I was, but I seem to have mislaid Aunt Tibby
again," she said candidly. "I'm afraid the Abbey was
built a thousand years too late to interest her. I stopped
for a moment to admire it and when I looked round she
was gone. To enter the Pump Room alone would be far

from proper, so I suppose I must go home for my abigail.''

"I'll be happy to offer my escort if it will save you from the frowns of the tabbies.''

"Thank you, sir, I believe that will serve, as we were introduced by no less a person than Mr. Guynette.'' She took his arm and they crossed the Pump Yard. "You are going to drink your daily pint, I expect?''

For a moment Matthew was taken aback, then he remembered the tale he had spun the night before to account for his presence in Bath. He coughed dramatically. It was an expert performance, for he had perfected it as a child as an excuse to escape from his tutor.

Miss Franklin looked worried. "I hope the waters will be of assistance. What a pity that your uncle's house is in North Parade, as the river mists surely cannot be good for a chest ailment.''

"On the contrary, ma'am,'' he invented rapidly as they entered the Pump Room. "The doctors tell me that dry air is of all things the most to be feared, since the tissues of the lungs are liable to become desiccated. The humidity by the Avon is precisely what is needed in such cases.''

"I'm very glad to hear it.''

Embarrassed by her obvious concern for his imaginary illness, he gestured at the busy scene before them. "You see, Miss Franklin, the place is not always haunted by valetudinarians. At this hour it is a fashionable promenade and meeting place for gossipmongers.''

"You terrify me.'' She laughed. "I should not care to be a subject of gossip.''

"Alas, no young lady of your beauty can hope to escape comment, but one so charming need not fear unfavourable comment—provided she avoids any appearance of forwardness," he said in a deliberately provocative tone.

She blushed in confusion, and he knew very well that she was thinking of their original encounter in the street. "I see the Barlows over there," she said in haste. "I must bid them good day."

They joined the merry group gathered round the sociable family. Plans were afoot to walk up Beechen Cliff that very afternoon.

"You will go with us, will you not, ma'am?" begged Mr. Barlow with what Matthew regarded as unnecessary eagerness. "We may not have another day so fine for ages, clear yet not too hot for the ladies."

"Pray do, Miss Franklin," seconded his sister.

"I shall be happy to join you," she said, "but surely, Miss Kitty, we agreed to be on Christian name terms. You must call me Jessica."

"Oh, yes, I'd like to. I was not perfectly sure... I did not wish to presume. I am very glad you are going to join us, Jessica. We shall meet at three at our lodgings, at 7, Westgate Buildings, if that is convenient? I hope you will bring Sir Nathan, too? And Mr. Walsingham, do you go with us? I vow the outing will be quite spoiled if you do not go with us."

Laughing at the attempted pout that ill suited Kitty's lively expression, Matthew acquiesced. No doubt the minx had hopes of keeping both him and Sir Nathan on a string, and he had noted also the silent, almost skeletal figure of Lord Peter Glossop standing by Mrs. Barlow's chair. Judging by their address in the Westgate Buildings, the Barlows were far from plump in the pocket and Miss Kitty must do the best she could for herself.

Mr. Barlow, too, was doubtless in the market for a wealthy spouse—and Jessica Franklin was laughing heartily at something he had just said to her. Matthew coughed.

She swung round at once. "Mr. Walsingham, you must drink your dose. Come, I shall go with you and make sure you don't shirk."

"Mama, you have not yet taken your glass today," Mr. Barlow observed. "I'll fetch it for you."

"Then I had best go with you, Bob," said Kitty with sisterly candour, "else you will likely forget it before you are half way across the room."

The four of them set out towards the pump, but the Barlows were waylaid by another acquaintance en route.

"I wonder whether Mrs. Barlow will ever receive her glassful," Jessica said with a smile as Matthew gave the attendant a shilling and accepted in return a tumbler of murky liquid.

"Lucky woman if she does not," he said gloomily. With her admonitory gaze fixed upon him, he braced himself and gulped the foul stuff down. "Ugh! No wonder it made poor Uncle Horace bilious." He shuddered.

"I would not drink it for the world," she admitted, "though it cannot possibly taste as horrid as it smells."

"That's what you think. You are mistaken, I assure you." In a mood for revenge, he happened to catch sight of the tongue-tied young lady he had danced with last night, just entering the Pump Room with her chaperone.

It would, in truth, have been difficult to miss her, since her green gown was embellished with a profusion of scarlet bows. However, far from making an effort to attract attention, Miss Pearson walked with head bowed, perhaps in contemplation of the ornate ruby brooch pinned to her bodice. Not to be foiled, for the second time that day Matthew ignored the gentlemanly code. "Miss Franklin, have you met Miss Pearson?"

Before she could respond, he led her up to the girl and her chaperone, a stout woman with an old-fashioned air. Startled, Miss Pearson cast him a nervous glance and curtsied as he performed the introductions.

"Miss Franklin, allow me to make you known to Miss Pearson and Mrs. Partridge."

"Woodcock! The Honourable Mrs. Woodcock," that lady corrected him sharply.

"I'm happy to make your acquaintance," said Jessica with aplomb. "I saw you at the Upper Rooms yesterday, I think. Did you enjoy the ball?"

Miss Pearson murmured something in which only the word "kind" was distinguishable.

"If it were not for Mr. Guynette's kindness, I should not have had a partner all evening, but it is sadly disconcerting to find oneself dancing with a total stranger, is it not?"

The girl raised shy brown eyes to Jessica's face and nodded eagerly. "I thought I was the only one to feel so, ma'am. How much more comfortable one is with people one knows."

"I daresay we shall both have friends aplenty in Bath in no time," Jessica encouraged her. "I hope you will count me your friend. Perhaps we might walk together in Sydney Gardens one afternoon?"

"I should like that of all things, ma'am." Miss Pearson smiled at last.

Matthew realized that she was really quite pretty, with her soft brown curls and delicate features. She was utterly lacking in countenance and taste, but with her obvious wealth to compensate for those deficiencies, she need not fear a dearth of suitors. Jessica, however, could have no ulterior motive for her kindness to the chit. The more he saw of Miss Franklin the better he liked her.

Having made arrangements to meet for a walk in the gardens, the young ladies parted.

"Congratulations, Miss Franklin," said Matthew. "You extracted more words from her in a couple of minutes than I did in the course of an entire set last night."

"Poor child, she is shockingly bashful. It was too bad of you to take her by surprise just now, and you need not pretend you did not have mischief in mind for I saw it in your eyes."

He laughed. "I only meant to punish you a little for forcing me to take my medicine. I expected to see you struggling in vain to hold a conversation. Since you succeeded, my plot was an absurd failure."

"You are an odious tease," she said reproachfully, but unable to hide her smile. "Oh dear, I wonder what has become of Aunt Tibby? I cannot wait here for her for ever."

"If you wish to return home, pray allow me to accompany you, ma'am."

"Will that be proper? I am not perfectly conversant with the niceties peculiar to Bath."

"Since I am acquainted with your brother and we are near neighbours, I doubt the most ardent stickler will see aught amiss."

"Well, I cannot think why I should take your word, sir, after the shocking disregard for propriety you have shown this morning, but thank you, I shall be glad of your escort."

Passing by the Abbey again, she glanced up at the angels on their ladder. The changed angle of the sun now made the figures stand out in sharp relief.

"I believe this will be the best time of day to sketch here," she said as they walked on. "I shall come back tomorrow at this hour, weather permitting."

"It sounds as if you are a serious artist," he said with some surprise.

"Heavens, no! I draw purely for my own pleasure, but of all the genteel accomplishments I was forced to acquire, it is the one I enjoy most."

"Then you must bring your sketch book this afternoon. The view of Bath from Beechen Cliff is famous."

"The trouble with distant prospects is that everything tends to fade into a haze. It takes a painter to do justice to a landscape. Is it far to Beechen Cliff?"

"Just across the river, where it swings to the west. There is a bridge at the end of Southgate Street. I daresay no more than half a mile as the crow flies, though the path winds up the steep part of the hill."

"I was thinking, sir—perhaps you might drive your curricle lest any of the ladies grow weary? Pray don't suppose that I mean myself," she added severely when he grinned. "Estates in the North are so large that I'm accustomed to riding ten miles across the fells to pay a morning call. An afternoon stroll is scarcely to be regarded as exercise."

"That is hardly an incentive to me to bring my curricle, if by driving I shall deprive myself of your company," he pointed out. "However, I'll have my groom bring it rather than risk having to carry some exhausted damsel home."

"As a matter of fact it was Mrs. Barlow I had in mind," she said, laughing, as they reached her front door. "Thank you for bringing me home, sir. I shall see you at the Westgate Buildings at three." She held out her hand and he bowed over it. A liveried footman opened the door and she entered without a backward glance.

Matthew walked back the few steps to his own front door in a thoughtful mood. Whatever she said, he was convinced that the suggestion about his curricle was due to her concern for himself. There was nothing he could do about his limp, but he was beginning to wish he had never yielded to the impulse to invent a lung injury.

He couldn't make up his mind whether to be gratified by her solicitude or annoyed by her presumption. He'd be damned if he'd let her bully him into drinking that foul water again!

CHAPTER SIX

"SUKEY! SUKEY, come quick. I'm going to wear the blue walking dress this afternoon and we must change the trim on my hat and parasol to match." Jessica sped up the stairs to her chamber.

The maid followed more slowly, wiping her hands on her grubby apron. It was that confusing never knowing whether she was housemaid, chambermaid or abigail, and a good job Ma had taught her to set her stitches neat as well as polish brass. She glanced back at Tad, crossing the hall below, and he winked at her. Right handsome he was in his livery, even if she knew that rolled up under the braided coat was the apron he wore for bringing in the coal. Lucky he saw Miss Jess had a gentleman with her in time to put on the coat afore he opened the door.

Still an' all, it was worth the masquerade if it meant Master Nathan—Sir Nathan as he was now—got to keep Langdale. There was no knowing which servants a new master would dismiss. 'Sides, it wouldn't be the same without Miss Jess. You couldn't ask for a better mistress.

"There's t'silk cornflowers I put in t'drawer, miss," she said, entering the chamber. "I can stick 'em on your hat in a trice and turn the brim down 'stead of up."

Jessica had already taken the new blue cambric gown from the wardrobe and was regarding it with approval.

"Yes, that will do very well. And I'll fashion a bow of blue ribbon to tie on the handle of the parasol. I'm glad I bought the white one after all."

"Mrs. Ancaster do say," observed Sukey as she unpicked the stitches fastening the apricot feather to the straw, "as gentlemen don't rightly notice what a lady's wearing so's she be neat and smart."

"I daresay, but the other ladies certainly do, and news would soon spread if I wore the same clothes to walk up Beechen Cliff as I did to parade in the Pump Room. I've no doubt gentlemen listen to rumour quite as avidly as ladies, even though they affect to despise it."

"Oh aye, t'menfolks is all gossips at heart. Why, wasn't our Tad out this morning on an errand for Mr. Hayes and come back full o' what Mr. Walsingham's valet told him."

"Mr. Walsingham's valet?"

"Aye, miss t'gentleman as walked you home just now." Sukey knew her mistress was dying to know what had been said but would not lower herself to ask. She took pity on her. "Seems as he's Viscount Stone's fav'rite nephew an' stands to inherit, for my lord has no nearer kin. He won't get no title, being as he's a sister's child, but house and land—Stone Gables 'tis called— an' all. A nice gentleman, is he, miss?"

"Oh, yes," said Jessica dreamily. "Very nice."

"Matthew his name is, Tad says."

"The valet's name?"

"No, he's Renfrew. Mr. Matthew Walsingham. And a very nice name, too, Miss Jessica."

Jessica smiled at her. "Why, I do believe you're teasing me, you wicked girl. I like him, but I only met him yesterday, after all, and I daresay I shall meet others I like as well."

"That's as may be, miss." Privately, Sukey doubted it. She was a romantic at heart, a believer in love at first sight. Hadn't she been faithful to Tad since the very first day she went to work at Langdale, when she was a twelve-year-old scullery maid and he a lad of sixteen?

Miss Jess was catched, she reckoned. Whether Mr. Matthew Walsingham was worthy of her remained to be seen.

At that moment, Sir Nathan was heard taking the stairs two at a time and calling his sister. "Jess? Can I come in? Tad says we have an invitation for this afternoon."

"The Barlows are walking up Beechen Cliff, with several others. Kitty Barlow particularly asked that I invite you to go too."

"She's the short, jolly girl, isn't she? Who else will be there?"

"Her brother, of course, and Lord Peter, I think. He was there. And a number of people whose names I don't know. Oh, and Mr. Walsingham." Jessica saw Sukey smile at this apparent afterthought and willed herself not to blush.

"Walsingham's going? I'll go with you then. You met him in the Pump Room?"

"Before I reached it. Tibby disappeared again and he kindly squired me there and coming home."

"Dash it, this obsession of Miss Tibbett's is becoming ridiculous. I'll have to have a word with her," he said, frowning.

"Pray don't, Nathan. She would be sadly mortified, and I'm not likely to come to any harm in the streets of Bath."

"It's all very well if you happen to meet up with a respectable gentleman like Walsingham, but supposing it had been Alsop?"

"Who is Alsop?"

Nathan flushed. "A fellow I met in the card room last night and called on this morning. He may be a baron but he's a bit of a Captain Sharp."

"You mean he cheats at cards?"

"I admit I wouldn't wish to introduce him to you, but you need not look at me so. Remember that I'm no pigeon for the plucking; I was in the army for three years."

"How do you suggest I avoid the acquaintance if he is a friend of yours?" Jessica kept her voice interested rather than reproachful and was rewarded with a rueful grin.

"Oh, very well, you win. I shall drop the acquaintance. He was not half so amusing this morning as last night, anyway. Walsingham's much more interesting to talk to, and there's nothing ramshackle about him. I'm going to ask Mrs. Ancaster for something to eat before we leave."

He dashed off. As Jessica changed into the blue gown and admired Sukey's transformation of her bonnet, she thought back over the conversation and found herself pleased with it.

In the first place, Nathan did not appear particularly attracted to Kitty Barlow, a delightful girl but from a worldly point of view not a desirable match. Secondly, he had the common sense to drop without a fuss an acquaintance whose friendship must damage his reputation if not his purse. And third—she smiled at herself in the glass as she tied the bow beneath her chin—third, but certainly not last, he liked Matthew Walsingham.

Humming "A North-Country maid," she went down to join him.

Miss Tibbett was sitting with him in the dining room, drinking tea while he consumed the remains of a sandwich. She looked rather self-conscious, and Jessica guessed that Nathan had taken her to task, though not too severely, as she was far from cast down. In spite of having asked him not to, she considered it showed an admirable sense of responsibility. It could not have been easy reminding his own former governess of her duty, but after all Tibby, however dear, was an employee, not an aunt. She really was shockingly vague.

Afraid that Tibby might feel it necessary to apologize, Jessica rushed into speech. "Have you heard about this afternoon's expedition? The view will be worth the climb, I believe."

"So I understand. I look forward to seeing it."

"Do you go with us then? I'm glad. Nathan, if you are quite sure you haven't missed a single crumb, we ought to leave or we shall keep the others waiting."

They were passing Number 9 when Mr. Walsingham stepped out of his front door and joined them. Nathan at once engaged him in conversation and the two of them dropped back a little, leaving the ladies to walk ahead except when there was a street to be crossed. Disappointed, Jessica persuaded herself that it was just as well—it would not do to be seen always on Mr. Walsingham's arm on such short acquaintance.

She had many opportunities that afternoon to remind herself of this philosophical conclusion. Mr. Barlow was determined to stay by her side. Annabel Forrester, a demure brunette with a languidly elegant air, promptly appropriated Mr. Walsingham, and Jessica had the doubtful felicity of hearing them talking and laughing behind her. Miss Forrester, she decided, had the most inane giggle she had ever heard, and Mr. Barlow was not nearly so amusing as she had thought him last night. Nonetheless, she contrived to appear as if she were enjoying herself immensely.

Kitty Barlow also appeared to be content with her lot though she was paired with Lord Peter. She chattered away, disregarding his silence and not bothering to strain her neck by peering up at his face. A heron keeping company with a perky little sparrow, Jessica thought, while Tibby and Mrs. Barlow were a blackbird and a plump turtledove. She tried to think of a similar comparison for Miss Forrester and Mr. Walsingham, but alas, they simply looked like a handsome, fashionable young couple.

Nathan had a red-head on his arm, Miss Maria Crane, a pert young lady with a dazzling repertoire of coy glances and flirtatious repartee. Eavesdropping, Jessica was surprised at how well her brother managed to keep up his end of the conversation, if conversation it could be called. He must have learned more than soldiering in America, among the Southern belles. He flashed her a glance of amused derision as he flattered Miss Crane with an extravagant compliment likening her copper locks to the sun rising in his heart.

When they reached the steep part of the hill, Mr. Barlow excused himself to assist his mother up the slope. Nathan was quick to offer his arm to "Aunt" Tibby, and after a momentary pout of disappointment, the red-head joined Jessica. She turned out to be quite sensible when she was not playing the coquette, and they had an interesting discussion of the use of perspective in sketching a landscape.

The view from Beechen Cliff was indeed superb. The entire party gathered in a group to admire it, and Jessica found herself beside Matthew Walsingham.

"I wish I had brought my sketch book after all," she said. "It would be worth the attempt, though I know my efforts would prove inadequate."

The hillside fell away to the Avon in the valley. On the other side of the river, the town spread its crescents and rows of honey-coloured stone terraces, punctuated by church spires and the Gothic magnificence of the Abbey. Beyond rose the green slope of Lansdown Hill.

"You can return another day to draw it," Mr. Walsingham pointed out. "I'd be happy to carry your paraphernalia for you."

"Oh yes, we must come again." Maria Crane materialized between them. "I shall ask Mama to organize a picnic and we shall have a sketching competition. Pray say you will be the judge, Mr. Walsingham?" She fluttered her eyelashes at him. Jessica was quite sure she had darkened them.

Kitty Barlow spoke to Jessica at that moment, and the next time she looked round Mr. Walsingham was firmly attached to the red-head. He gave Jessica a wry smile and raised his shoulders a fraction of an inch in a hint of a helpless shrug, but that was little consolation when she heard him plying Maria with compliments as outrageous as Nathan's. How did the girl manage to elicit such nonsense from usually sane males?

At least, Jessica was glad to note, Mr. Walsingham's slight limp didn't appear to be any the worse for the exercise. Nor had she heard him coughing, though Mrs. Barlow was decidedly breathless after climbing the hill.

Walking back down the slope, they found Mr. Walsingham's curricle waiting where the path met the lane leading to the bridge. Miss Tibbett volunteered to chaperone the young people so that the groom could drive a grateful Mrs. Barlow back to her lodgings.

"You'll all come in for a dish of tea, I hope," she invited as Mr. Walsingham handed her into his carriage. "The kettle will be on the boil by the time you reach Westgate Buildings. Thank you, sir, so kind, and such a splendid vehicle. Why, I shall be the envy of everyone." She beamed and waved as the curricle rolled down the hill.

It was impossible not to like the Barlows. Jessica chose to walk the rest of the way with Kitty rather than demean herself by a deliberate attempt to catch Matthew Walsingham, now that he was momentarily free. She was rewarded when he made use of that moment to escape from Miss Crane. He offered Miss Tibbett his arm and listened with obliging respect to a lecture on Roman architecture.

"A charming young man," Miss Tibbett announced when at last they returned to 15, North Parade, "and he even asked intelligent questions."

"I'm meeting him tomorrow morning to go for a spin in the curricle," Nathan added.

As she went up to her chamber to change for dinner, Jessica wondered whether Mr. Walsingham preferred a demure damsel like Annabel Forrester or a coy flirt like Maria Crane. After managing Langdale for two years, she knew herself incapable of playing either part with conviction, even to compete for Mr. Walsingham's attention.

With what high hopes of the afternoon she had earlier descended the same stairs, merrily humming a tune. She should have remembered the third line of the verse: "She wept and she sighed and she bitterly cried."

No, it had not been bad enough for that. Laughing at herself, she sang, "The oak and the ash and the bonny ivy tree, they flourish at home in my own country."

"Had a good time, did you?" asked Sukey indulgently.

"Yes, I did," Jessica said, surprised to realize that it was true. After all, Mr. Matthew Walsingham, whatever her designs upon him, was as yet no more than a pleasant acquaintance.

The Franklins and Miss Tibbett spent the evening at home. They could not afford to gad about every night and, as Miss Tibbett pointed out, if people became accustomed to seeing them do so, it would occasion comment when they did not.

"Let them suppose that we prefer a peaceful evening now and then," she advised, "and no one will think twice about it."

She and Nathan settled down to a game of chess, while Jessica fetched her sketch book and practised drawing the prospect from Beechen Cliff from memory. If the picnic and sketching contest actually came about, she intended to be prepared. She had not cared for the confident gleam in Maria Crane's eyes when she proposed it.

The next day she took her sketch book with her when she set off for the Pump Room. As she expected to meet some of her new friends there, Tibby was excused from attendance. Instead, Sukey pattered along at her side, leaving a disgruntled Tad to dust the parlour.

After an hour or so chatting and strolling about the Pump Room with Kitty, Maria, and Annabel, Jessica collected Sukey and went out to draw the Abbey. They found a conveniently placed stone bench. The maid was quite content to sit in the warm sun watching the passers-by while her mistress busied herself with pencil and paper.

Jessica had scarcely blocked in the outlines of the octagonal tower and made a start on the first angel when she became aware of a presence behind her.

"A good beginning," said Mr. Walsingham approvingly. "You have an eye for proportion."

She glanced up at him, smiling a welcome. "I like drawing buildings. They don't move, like people and animals, and they don't fade into the distance like views. Have you yet taken the waters today, sir?"

"Well, no, not yet," he admitted, looking sheepish. "I was..." His words were interrupted by a racking cough.

"You were just on your way to the Pump Room," she prompted.

"As a matter of fact, what I was going to say is that I was hoping to give you a tour of the Abbey first."

"And then conveniently forget your medicine afterwards? Shame on you, Mr. Walsingham."

"Very well, ma'am, I shall go and drink a glass if you promise to wait here until I return."

"Since the light and shadow are just as I want them, I can safely promise—unless you fall in with Miss Forrester or Miss Crane and forget the passage of time."

He blenched. "Are they both in the Pump Room? *Must* I go in there?"

"You must, sir." It would be interesting, Jessica thought, to see if the young ladies she was beginning to consider rivals would prevail despite his apparent dismay. If he preferred their company to hers, nothing in the world could make her pursue him however rich his uncle and however desperate her straits.

"You are cruel, fair maid," he said with a sigh, "but behold, I obey."

Was she quite shatterbrained, Jessica wondered, to send him away? Even if he liked her better than the others, a visit to a church could hardly compete with the attractions of the fashionable gathering in the Pump Room. Very much aware of the passing minutes, she returned to the angels on their ladders to heaven.

CHAPTER SEVEN

WHAT WAS JESSICA Franklin about? Matthew wondered. Was she really so concerned for his health that she would risk losing his company, or did she simply not value his company as much as he had hoped? He didn't think she was so sure of herself as to suppose she could simply crook her little finger and have him come running.

Yesterday afternoon had been unbelievably frustrating. He had hoped for a chance to get to know Jessica better, and instead he had been forced to entertain two young ladies as silly as any he had ever met. Miss Tibbett's knowledgeable dissertation had been fascinating in comparison, especially sweetened by the fact that she was Jessica's aunt and chaperone.

Entering the Pump Room, Matthew glanced swiftly around and spotted the group he wanted to avoid. He made his way, via the opposite end of the room, to the door on the far side and out to the baths. There he lingered for as long as he could bear the sulphurous fumes before he hurried back past the danger point, breathing a sigh of relief as he reached the entrance unaccosted.

He stepped out and gulped the fresh air. Jessica was still there, sitting with her back to him, to all appearances utterly absorbed in her drawing. The dashing straw hat with the curly pink feather, matching the rosebuds on her gown, revealed more of her extraordinary hair than the blue-flowered one she had worn the day before. Nonetheless, Matthew wished she would take it off altogether. He wanted to see the sunlight play on those flaxen tresses.

Despite her apparent concentration she must have heard his uneven footsteps, for she looked round as he approached.

"Oh dear, you look alarmingly queasy."

"You are flattering, Miss Franklin!"

His response brought forth her enchanting laugh. "I merely wondered whether your doctor is right in thinking the waters will be of benefit to your health. It would be a pity if the remedy for your chest proved detrimental to your digestion. Perhaps you take after your uncle."

"Heaven forbid! Not that Uncle Horace isn't a splendid fellow in his way," he added hastily, "but I'd hate to have inherited his dyspepsia. Perhaps I'd better stop drinking the stuff in case you're right. Now that's enough on the subject or I shall take to my bed. Shall we go into the Abbey?"

"Yes, I have made a good start on my sketch. Sukey, will you carry these, if you please? You may wait here or come with us into the church, as you choose."

The abigail elected to stay outside. Matthew offered Jessica his arm and they strolled from the bright sun into the cool dimness of the Abbey church. Jessica gasped.

"I didn't realize it would be so different from Durham Cathedral, so light and airy, reaching up as if it were about to soar into the sky."

"I've never been to Durham, but it's Romanesque, isn't it? The Normans built solidly."

"Yes, the cathedral gives an impression of weight. The windows are smaller and all the pillars are decorated, not elegantly simple like these."

"Rounded arches with pillars as wide as the openings, instead of the pointed arches, slender pillars and delicate tracery of the Perpendicular that you see here. The Abbey is one of the last of the Gothic cathedrals, built in the sixteenth century. Henry VII's architect, William Vertue, designed the most marvellous fan vaulting for the roof—I've seen the drawings—but it was never constructed."

"You seem to know a great deal about the subject." Jessica sounded surprised and curious.

"I've always been interested in architecture," Matthew said rather self-consciously. "Just as a hobby, of course. I'm sorry, I didn't mean to bore you with a lecture."

"I didn't find it boring. I know very little about anything later than Roman architecture, since Aunt Tibbett, who supervised my education, considers anything built after *anno Domini* 100 to be decadent. I know all about temples and amphitheatres and Hadrian's Wall, and I could draw you a plan of a hypocaust."

"Er, what's a hypocaust when it's at home? When I was a schoolboy learning Latin we never studied anything but battles."

"The Roman system of hot air heating."

"And you could draw it? Some architects today are designing complete heating systems for houses, and I should like to see how the Romans managed it."

"I'll see what I can do," she promised.

"What an amazing girl you are. Have you any other unusual talents I've not yet discovered?"

"Oh, no. Apart from the Romans in Britain, my education was thoroughly conventional. I play the pianoforte and the harp, and sing a little; speak French, not very well; embroider exquisitely; and write poetry to order."

Matthew laughed. "A very paragon of genteel accomplishments. Your sketching, at least, is good beyond the ordinary, judging by what I saw of your angels on the ladder."

"Thank you, kind sir." Dimpling, she bobbed a curtsy. "And that reminds me that poor Sukey will be wondering what has become of us."

"I'll return you to your abigail if you will promise to stand up with me at tonight's assembly."

"A promise made under duress is no promise," she pointed out. "But yes, I shall save you a dance if you wish."

"I do wish. And will you drive with me tomorrow afternoon?" he requested as they emerged into the sunshine and stood blinking a moment on the threshold. "Mrs. Barlow can assure you that mine is a thoroughly respectable vehicle."

"Thank you, sir, but I am engaged to walk with Miss Pearson in Sydney Gardens," she said, sounding regretful yet oddly relieved.

Recovering from the dazzling brightness, he noted the heightened colour in her cheeks. She was absurdly sensitive about his curricle, he thought with an inward smile. One of these days, when he handed her into the carriage, he would tell her that of course he had recognized her, and had not for a moment thought her backward glance impertinent.

"I WISH I HAD NOT ASKED Miss Pearson to walk with me today," Jessica said wistfully to Miss Tibbett as they crossed Pulteney Bridge. "If I had only known that Mr. Walsingham was going to invite me to drive with him."

"It was the kind thing to do, and from what you have said of the child it sounds as if she is sadly in need of kindness."

"Not so much kindness, I believe, as encouragement. Careful, Tibby, you will be run down." She pulled her companion back onto the pavement as a barouche swept into Laura Place. "Gracious heaven! That carriage quite casts Mr. Walsingham's into the shade."

The vehicle in question, drawn by a pair of showy greys, was painted in eggshell blue with gold curlicues, and the coachman on the box was clad in matching livery. For all Jessica knew it might pass without notice in Hyde Park, but in staid Bath it commanded the attention of everyone in sight as it drew to a halt beside her.

She glanced up to find Miss Pearson looking down at her anxiously.

"Miss Franklin, I'm dreadfully sorry," she said with a sort of half gasp. "We should have fetched you from home."

Jessica smiled at her. "Being country bred, we like to walk," she said, "but since you are here it would be foolish indeed to refuse to be taken up. Good day, Mrs. Par...er, Woodcock."

As she and Aunt Tibby stepped up into the carriage, the Honourable Mrs. Woodcock bowed graciously and remarked upon the fineness of the weather. The conversation continued along the same lines, Miss Pearson remaining silent, as the barouche started off again and rumbled along Great Pulteney Street to the Sydney Gardens.

The ladies descended by the pavilion, named for some obscure reason after Admiral Holburne of Menstrie, and entered the gardens. Green lawns and gravel paths rose in a gentle slope up Bathwick Hill, with scattered groups of trees and shrubs to lend variety to the prospect. Across this rural background paraded the white or pale pastel gowns and gay parasols of strolling ladies, the blue or brown coats of their escorts.

Jessica was horridly aware that Miss Pearson's vivid violet dress was bound to draw as many eyes as her carriage. Gracious heaven, the girl was even wearing an amethyst necklace for a walk in the park. Determined not to show her embarrassment, Jessica linked arms with her and chose a path that seemed less frequented than most.

"I've not been here before," she said as their chaperones dropped behind. "What a delightful place to take the air."

"Is it not? Papa says Hyde Park is far more fashionable and much larger, but it is always excessively crowded and people stare so."

"You have lived in London?"

"All my life, except when I was at school. I was perfectly happy there until Papa took it into his head that I must make my bow to Society. That's why he hired Mrs. Woodcock to chaperone me. He thought that as an 'Honourable' she would be able to introduce me to the right people, but it was all a hum."

"It was?" Jessica asked cautiously. Quiet, shy Miss Pearson appeared to be ready to open the floodgates to a torrent of confidences.

"Yes, for though her father was a baron, she was married to a clergyman and never set foot in London for thirty years. We only went to one party all Season, and that was horrid. No one spoke to us. So this year Papa decided to buy a house in Bath."

"And do you like Bath better?"

"Well, it's true that I go to all the balls and I have danced with any number of gentlemen, but I never know what to say to them. And I hate sitting with Mrs. Woodcock, waiting for Mr. King or Mr. Guynette to find me a partner and never sure whether the partners they find really want to dance with me at all."

"I know what you mean. I felt that way at my first assembly."

"Mrs. Woodcock says some gentlemen ask for an introduction only because they know I am rich. She told Papa that Mr. Barlow and Lord Alsop are fortune hunters. Of course I know Sir Nathan is not, nor Mr. Walsingham. He is Lord Stone's heir, and Lord Stone is almost as rich as Papa, but I always feel that Mr. Walsingham is laughing at me and I cannot be comfortable with him."

Jessica's guilt at the girl's trust in Nathan's respectability gave way to uneasiness as she recognized the name of the "Captain Sharp" her brother had mentioned. She herself had danced with Lord Alsop once and managed to avoid him thereafter. A gaunt gentleman of perhaps fifty years, he had a dissipated look about him, and a manner at once leering and ingratiating. His dandified dress, with high shirt points, padded shoulders and wasp waist, did nothing to counteract the unpleasant impression he had made on her. Though she considered herself more than a match for him, she could easily imagine him persecuting Miss Pearson with his attentions.

"The assemblies are much more fun if you know some young ladies to talk to between the sets," she said. "Will you sit with me at the next ball?"

"Oh, Miss Franklin, that would be beyond anything!"

Jessica smiled at her, a little overwhelmed by her gratitude. If they were to sit together, she decided, something must be done about the vulgarity of her dress. Though old-fashioned, Mrs. Woodcock's gown was decently black, as became a widow. Perhaps "Papa" was responsible for the appalling lack of taste.

"I have not met Mr. Pearson at the assemblies or in the Pump Room. He is not an invalid, I trust?"

"No, he..." she hesitated, then went on in a burst of candour "...he does not go because he does not want to spoil my chances. You see, he is what people of your station call a Cit." Her eyes were huge with apprehension.

"Ah, that explains a good deal," said Jessica slowly, patting her hand. "Cheer up, I shall not immediately cut the acquaintance, you know. But if your father wishes you to make a good marriage, you must not be so free with your confidences."

"Oh no, I have not told anyone else. I feel...I felt right away that I could trust you. But Papa does not mean to keep it a secret, only not to seem encroaching. He is already well known in Bath among the better class of merchants. In fact, before he retired he used to do business with one of the aldermen."

Feeling in need of time to sort out this flood of information, Jessica was delighted to see her brother and Mr. Walsingham crossing a lawn towards them. They were an attractive pair, Nathan not tall but with the proud carriage of a soldier, his gold hair gleaming in the sun as he raised his hat in greeting; and Matthew Walsingham lean and broad-shouldered, his limp in no way impairing the jauntiness of his stride.

"Good day, ladies," said Matthew, grinning. "What a surprise to meet you here."

"It is indeed," Jessica riposted, "since I was under the impression that you intended to spend the afternoon driving some fortunate young lady in your curricle."

"I *hoped* to drive a *certain* young lady, ma'am. Failing that, I hope to show her the sights of Sydney Gardens. Have you yet climbed the hill as far as the canal? Then allow me, pray, to escort you thither."

She glanced at Nathan and Miss Pearson. Her brother shrugged and raised his eyes to heaven, then offered the timid young lady his arm. Jessica turned to the chaperones. They professed themselves perfectly content to await their charges on a nearby bench, so she took Matthew's arm and they started up the hill.

Following behind, Nathan was disgruntled. When he agreed to go with Walsingham to the gardens, he had not expected to be left to entertain the silent Miss Pearson. He had danced with her once, but it was easy to dance without talking. A speechless stroll in the park was ridiculous.

"Are you enjoying the entertainments of Bath, ma'am?" he enquired, making a conscientious effort.

"Oh yes, sir. At least, I shall now that I have met your sister. I believe she is the kindest person in the world."

Nathan blinked at the unexpectedly enthusiastic reply. "She's a great gun," he said vaguely, "and deuced clever, too. Did you know she managed my estate for me while I was in the army?"

The girl's face filled with awe, but not, it turned out, at Jessica's accomplishment. "You were in the army? How very brave you must be!"

"Well, I don't know about that," he demurred with becoming modesty. She was a taking little thing after all, with those big brown eyes and that soft brown hair. It was a pity she was dressed with such excruciating vulgarity. "One does what one has to."

"To save us all from Boney."

"Actually, I was in America."

"Fighting Red Indians?" She was breathless at the thought, hanging on his arm as if she were afraid a horde of savages lurked in ambush behind the next tree.

"Most of them were on our side, as a matter of fact. We were fighting ordinary American soldiers. Actually, I think the war was quite unnecessary," he confessed, wondering even as he spoke why he was revealing to Miss Pearson what he had not even told Jess. "They are our brothers and ought to be our friends. The last battle I was in, at New Orleans, took place after the peace treaty had been signed—can you think of anything stupider? I wish I had been in the Peninsula!"

"A soldier cannot choose where to go," she consoled him, with an oddly enchanting air of mingled wisdom and anxiety. "You did your duty, and wherever you were, it was very brave of you."

They had reached one of the bridges over the Kennet-Avon Canal. Jessica and Walsingham were waiting for them, leaning on the ornamental iron railing to watch a string of barges pass underneath. Nathan was struck by how comfortable they were with each other. Perhaps his sister's plan was not so outrageous after all, if it meant she was going to marry Walsingham. He could not think of anyone he had rather have for a brother-in-law.

"Miss Franklin has agreed to entrust herself to me in a boat on the canal one of these days," Walsingham greeted them. "Are you brave enough to join us, Franklin?"

"Sir Nathan is brave enough for *anything,*" said Miss Pearson, shy but firm.

"I am indeed, ma'am," he said, smiling down at her, "if you will venture with me."

She blushed and nodded. After settling on a day for the outing, they all turned to admire the view of the town, then started back down the hill.

Nathan was racking his brains. Miss Pearson was far too charming a young lady to be allowed to continue wearing gowns garish—if not décolleté—enough for an actress. As a gentleman, he could not decently make any suggestions, but perhaps Jess could manage something.

As they approached Tibby and Mrs. Woodcock, he said in a low voice, "Miss Pearson, if you wish to repay my sister for any kindness she has done you, perhaps you would go shopping with her. My aunt has not the least interest in fashions and fripperies and I know Jess would be glad of a companion."

"I should be happy to accompany Miss Franklin," she said diffidently.

"Jessica! I have been telling Miss Pearson how you love to shop and are always complaining that Aunt Tibby will not go with you."

"Indeed, it is a sad trial to me," his sister responded, meeting his eye with a quizzical look.

He gave the girl a gentle nudge.

"If you do not mind, ma'am, I will go with you one day."

"A splendid notion," Jessica said cordially. "I am in grave need of a bonnet I noticed in Milsom Street. Are you free tomorrow morning?"

Silently blessing her, Nathan treated everyone to tea in the Holburne of Menstrie pavilion.

Later, when they met at dinner, he thanked his sister for her cooperation.

"Just what was going on there?" asked Miss Tibbett suspiciously. "You know I am always perfectly willing to go shopping with you, Jessica."

"I know, dear Tibby, but if I am not mistaken, Nathan has more in mind than a simple shopping expedition."

"I hoped you might be able to influence Miss Pearson's taste," he admitted. "If you insist on befriending her, it will be easier on our eyes if she is more . . . er, *demurely* clad."

"Precisely my own feeling," she agreed, looking at him knowingly. "It is a shame to hide her light under a bushel, for she is a pretty child, is she not?"

He concentrated on carving the roast saddle of mutton. "Is she?" he asked. "I scarcely noticed."

CHAPTER EIGHT

"*I* NEVER HAD THE MAKING of them gowns, miss," Madame Guinevere assured Jessica as her assistant led Miss Pearson to a fitting room. "You may be sure of that. It's my belief them London modistes'll do anything if you pay 'em enough. A crying shame, I call it, putting the poor young lady in colours as 'd embarrass a peacock." She bustled after them, calling for the lavender dimity.

Jessica would have liked to take her young friend to her own seamstress, but she suspected that the unknown Mr. Pearson would despise any but the most expensive modiste in Bath. At least Madame's front shop was comfortable. While she waited, she looked through the latest issue of *Ackermann's Repository of Arts, Literature, Commerce, Manufactures, Fashions and Politics*. The section on fashion was the only one to show signs of wear.

Not ten minutes later she was called into the fitting room to give her opinion. Miss Pearson was clad in a white muslin walking dress with coquelicot ribbons threaded around the sleeves, hem and bodice, and a coquelicot sash at the high waist.

"Is it all right, Miss Franklin?" she asked anxiously. "Papa does so like bright colours."

"Charming." Jessica noted the bloom in her cheeks, which had seemed pale in comparison to her garish

dress. She really was very pretty. "It suits you to per-
fection."

The girl twisted to look in the mirror.

"Careful!" advised Madame Guinevere. "Them
pins'll fall out. I can have it ready for you in a half hour,
miss."

"I'll take it," said Miss Pearson decisively.

"And while we are waiting you can try on a few
more," Jessica suggested. "The lavender dimity would
make a splendid carriage dress."

An hour later the young ladies were about to emerge
from the shop, when Lucy—they were on Christian
name terms by then—tugged on Jessica's arm.

"Oh, pray wait a moment. There is that horrid Lord
Alsop passing by."

Jessica was only too pleased to comply. Lucy must
stop wearing a king's ransom in jewels, Jessica thought,
then she would not be viewed as fair prey by every fortune hunter in Bath. For once she quite forgot that Nathan was one of their number.

"Have you any pearls?" she asked. "They would go
best with your new primrose ball dress."

"No, Papa never cared for pearls."

"Perrin's is next door, but I suppose your pin money
will not stretch to such a purchase."

"I have enough money," Lucy assured her, "only I
think I ought not to buy jewellery without consulting
Papa. You see, he was a jeweller before he retired, or
rather, a wholesale importer of precious stones and gold
and silver."

"And he does not care for pearls? Come, Lord Alsop is gone. Our next stop is the milliner, and then, I
believe, it is time I had a word with Mr. Pearson."

The jewel merchant had bought one of the larger houses in the Circus, in a part of the town to which Jessica had not previously penetrated. She admired the three curved terraces encircling a central open space, with their paired pillars between the windows, carved stone frieze, and ornamental ironwork. As befitted the elegance of the building, the Pearsons' dignified butler was haughtily impassive. Not by so much as a blink did he suggest that he had noticed the change in his young mistress's appearance.

Jessica decided she preferred dear old Hayes, with his wrinkled jowls and his devotion to the family.

Lucy led the way into a comfortable sitting room which smelled faintly of tobacco. In a chair by the table in the window sat a short, lean man, soberly dressed, reading a newspaper. He appeared to be in his sixties, considerably older than Jessica had expected.

"Papa," said Lucy.

"It's a terrible business, this in Belgium," he said, still studying his paper. "We must hope Wellington can pull us through." Then he looked up and sprang to his feet. "Why, I didn't know you'd brought a friend with you, puss."

Lucy performed the introductions, her father rubbing his hands and bowing repeatedly with an air of satisfaction.

"I take it right kindly in you, miss, to be inviting our Lucy to walk with you and all," he said, beaming. "I see you've been doing some shopping, puss." He chucked his daughter under the chin.

"Yes, Papa, do you like it?"

"It's well enough, I daresay, but it's not what I'd choose. I like a bit of colour on a young thing."

Lucy's face fell. "I have ordered several more. Shall I cancel the orders?"

"Certainly not." Jessica decided it was time to take a hand. "Lucy, I should like a word in private with your papa."

He gave her a hard look, his genial expression becoming noncommittal. Lucy kissed his cheek and pattered out of the room. Not waiting to be invited, Jessica took a seat at the table and waved to him to join her.

"Sir, I can see that you love your daughter. Surely you cannot be so cruel as to make her wear clothes that are quite unsuited to both her years and the station to which you wish her to aspire. In company, Lucy stands out like a purple thistle among lilies."

He gave an involuntary snort of laughter, then glared at her. "I don't wish my girl to fade into the background. Modern fashions are downright wishy-washy."

"Nonetheless, a young lady who wishes to be accepted by Society must follow the modes. What is more, the paler colours suit Miss Pearson much better. Did you not notice her rosy cheeks just now?"

"Aye," he said grudgingly, "she looked right pretty, but to my eye she always does."

"Let her keep her new gowns, I beg of you. She will be much more comfortable if her clothes do not attract impertinent stares."

"You've got something there." He gave a martyred sigh. "I daresay the chit will want a whole new wardrobe."

Sensing capitulation, Jessica smiled. "And a string of pearls. They are really the only jewellery proper for a young girl, besides simple beads."

"Beads!" Mr. Pearson unexpectedly exploded, thumping the table. "Lucy has some of the finest gems in the country—in the world!"

"And she shall proudly wear them when she is an established matron. Do you *want* elderly roués like Lord Alsop gathering about her like flies around a honey-pot?"

"Pearls?" he asked in a small voice.

"Pearls. And a single strand, not some elaborate collar such as dowagers wear to hide their scrawny necks."

"Pearls it is. She'll have the finest matched set in the country. I'll have Jack Perrin find 'em for me."

"Earrings are acceptable," Jessica conceded graciously, "and perhaps a second string to twine in her hair. Strictly for the ballroom, mind!"

He reached across the table and patted her cheek, just as Lucy returned, followed by Mrs. Woodcock and a tea tray borne by a footman in eggshell blue and gold. For a moment Jessica wondered whether to suggest that Mr. Pearson repaint his barouche in some nice conventional colour like maroon. She decided enough had been accomplished for one day.

Half an hour later, the blue, gold-curlicued barouche returned her to North Parade. Nathan happened to arrive at the same moment.

"Well?" he enquired as he handed her down.

"Wait and see," she said smugly. She had no intention of telling him that Lucy's papa was a Cit, but she felt he needed some explanation for the girl's oddities. "Mrs. Woodcock has not been in Society for thirty years, it seems, and her notions of what is suitable for a debutante are positively Gothick. Lucy is lucky to have avoided being forced into hoops!"

"You have been successful, I collect. Well, I shan't make you wait for my news. I went round to see Walsingham this morning..."

"What a surprise. You do so every day, do you not?"

"You really must get out of this habit of interrupting a fellow!" He opened the front door and followed her in, dropping his hat and gloves on the hall table. "I'm sure it's deuced unladylike. As I was trying to say, he showed me some drawings he's been doing—plans, I suppose you'd call them—and he mentioned that you had expressed an interest. Being a bachelor he can't properly invite you to his house, so I asked him to dine with us and bring the plans for you to see."

"To dine! Gracious heavens, I must consult Mrs. Ancaster. It is late in the day for marketing. And you must ask Hayes for suggestions about wines and send Tad out to buy what's needed. And Sukey must press my blue silk, and I must make sure Aunt Tibby is not planning to spend the evening with her retired clergyman and his wife, and..."

Nathan laughed. "I didn't mean to throw you into high fidgets. I hope I know better than to spring such a thing on you at the last moment—I invited him for tomorrow."

"Wretch!" she said, hugging him. "Why did you not say so sooner? We absolutely *must* put on a good show."

JESSICA BEGAN HER preparations early the next day. Everything must be quite perfect, and in view of their minimal staff she and Nathan and Tibby all had to lend a hand. For several hours the household was at sixes and sevens, but by the time she went up to change for dinner, order was emerging from chaos. The dining room table gleamed with crystal and silver on a snowy cloth, and appetizing aromas drifted from the nether regions, where Mrs. Ancaster was putting forth her best efforts.

"You'd think it was the Prince Regent hisself coming to dinner," she grumbled to Sukey as she added a last pinch of seasoning to the gravy. "Here, taste this." She held out a wooden spoon.

"Mmm, that's one o' your best for sure, Mrs. Ancaster. Mr. Walsingham's more important to Miss Jess nor any prince," the maid replied, and they exchanged a look of complicity.

His livery coat freshly sponged, Tad was stationed in the hall. The moment the door knocker sounded he sprang to open the door, and as Mr. Walsingham stepped across the threshold, Hayes appeared as if by magic to usher him into the drawing room. The butler found himself with a bedewed bottle of chilled champagne in each hand.

"Sir?" he said, startled.

"Haven't you heard the news?"

The commotion his report elicited was audible in the drawing room, but when he entered Jessica pretended she had not heard it. She looked up, rose and came forward to greet him, surprised by his look of elation.

"Miss Franklin, have you not heard the news?" He took both her hands in his, beaming. "Miss Tibbett, your servant, ma'am. Franklin—it's victory! Old Hookey has rompéd the Corsican and sent him scurrying with his tail between his legs!"

In the astonished pause which followed, a sound like a gunshot was heard from the dining room next door. A moment later Hayes came through the connecting door with a silver tray of champagne glasses full of sparkling golden liquid. How fortunate, thought Jessica as she raised hers in a toast to the Duke of Wellington, that the house came equipped with the correct glasses for every occasion.

Naturally the talk at dinner was all of Napoleon's defeat, the two former soldiers bemoaning their absence from the conflict. Nonetheless, Mr. Walsingham did full justice to Mrs. Ancaster's good, plain North-country cooking.

"My compliments to your cook," he said when the ladies withdrew at the end of the meal, then added with a teasing look in his grey eyes, "and tell her that I hope to be invited again."

"Next time Wellington defeats Bonaparte," Jessica promised saucily, with a giggle that she put down to the champagne going to her head.

As if he had read her mind, Hayes immediately brought tea to the drawing room. Tibby, who had partaken sparingly of the bubbling nectar, poured her a cup, and after she drank it her mind cleared.

"Thank you," she said gratefully to Hayes as he removed the tray. "I hope you and the others will drink to the victory with one of the bottles we bought for this evening."

The butler's sagging jowls stretched in a smile. "Thank you, Miss Jessica, I already took the liberty of pouring us each a small glass, knowing you wouldn't mind on such a great occasion. We'll finish up the bottle later, when all's done that needs doing."

The gentlemen joined them a few minutes later. Mr. Walsingham came straight to sit beside Jessica on the brocaded sofa.

"Do you know, in the excitement I quite forgot the house plans. Your brother has sent your footman to fetch them. I hope you will not be disappointed—it is no grand mansion I have designed, merely a hunting box.''

"With Aunt Tibby's expert assistance I have sketched a hypocaust for you.''

He examined her drawing with interest, comparing the Roman under-floor system to what he knew of hot air systems installed at Pakenham Hall, in Ireland, and Coleshill in Berkshire. Then Tad arrived with the building plans and they all moved into the dining room, by now cleared of dishes, and spread the papers on the table.

Jessica's first interest was a depiction of the façade. She liked the informal modern asymmetry of it, and the huge windows that Mr. Walsingham said would look downhill to a stream, but there was something stark about it. Then she realized that there were no shadows, no trees or bushes to soften the outlines.

"It's an elevation, not a work of art,'' he explained. He had found in her sketch book her drawing of the Abbey and was looking from that to his own in a dissatisfied way. "I don't know how to do all the shading and stuff that you do to make it look attractive, not just accurate.''

"I'd be happy to make an attempt at it,'' Jessica said tentatively. "I'm not sure if I could do it without the building itself in front of me, but if you like . . . ?''

"Will you? Will you really? That would be splendid. There's a wood behind the house, and Lord Ilfracombe was talking of putting in gardens in front, just something simple as it's only for the hunting season.''

"Lord Ilfracombe?'' enquired Nathan.

"He asked me to give him some ideas for building on a piece of land he bought in Leicestershire.''

"So this is not purely theoretical," Jessica said, pulling a ground floor plan towards her. "This room must be the one with the windows facing the stream, is it not? You have it marked as a library. I would put the drawing room there—oh, but you have no drawing room on this floor."

"That's because drawing rooms are for ladies," Nathan told her, "and gentlemen don't invite females to their hunting boxes. Or at least, only..."

He broke off, and Jessica saw Matthew Walsingham give him a warning glance. She looked from one to the other with interest.

"Only?"

"Never mind!" said her brother hastily, and their guest diverted her to a discussion of his ideas for the servants' quarters.

"Only demimondaines," Miss Tibbett whispered to her a moment later, when Mr. Walsingham was explaining something to Nathan.

Jessica grinned at her. "That," she said softly, "was perfectly obvious."

Tibby shook her head in reproof.

At last they had studied and discussed every aspect of Lord Ilfracombe's hunting box. Mr. Walsingham collected his papers, leaving the sheet with the elevation for Jessica to copy.

"For an amateur, you have gone to a lot of trouble over this," she remarked, ringing for the tea tray.

"If something is worth doing, it's worth doing well." He looked oddly self-conscious as he uttered this cliché. "Besides, Ilfracombe is a good friend of mine."

They went through to the drawing room for tea. Then Matthew Walsingham took his leave and the others accompanied him into the hall. Tad opened the front door. The evening mist from the river was creeping up the street like a housebreaker, peering in at ground floor windows and sneaking down area steps.

"I shall walk with you," said Jessica impulsively. "I need some fresh air." She stepped out.

"Jessica, your bonnet!" protested Miss Tibbett.

She waved dismissively. "I'm only going a hundred yards." She set off, and Matthew hurried after her. They walked side by side through the cool, damp night, not touching, not speaking.

"Tad, take a lantern and light the way," Nathan ordered, although between street lamps and house lights there was no dearth of illumination.

The footman grabbed a lantern from a hook by the door and lit it from a candle on the hall table.

Glancing back, Matthew saw him following, and beyond him the bright rectangle of the doorway of Number 15, with two watching figures silhouetted. He grinned to himself. Jessica's independent spirit was not to be curbed by brother or aunt.

They reached his house and he turned towards her to say good night. Beads of mist glistened in her moon-pale hair, haloing her shadowed face. Suddenly he wanted to kiss her—and only the footman's presence stopped him.

But after all, that was undoubtedly what Tad was there for.

CHAPTER NINE

MATTHEW WOKE THE NEXT morning to a rainy day, the first since his arrival in Bath. After breakfast he settled down to design a heating system for Lord Ilfracombe's hunting box. Most of the work on his plans had been done while he was confined to bed by his mangled leg. Ilfracombe had liked what he had seen and had encouraged him to finish the project. Matthew had scarcely glanced at the plans, though, for the past six months until, arriving in Bath, he had returned to them as a possible means of subsistence and completed the work despite grave doubts of its worth. The Franklins' enthusiasm last night had renewed his faith in his ability and sparked new ideas.

Recalling Jessica's reaction to the lack of a drawing room, he grinned, then his smile grew tender at the memory of her walking at his side through the mist. Was he in love? Could life possibly be so kind as to allow him to fall for a girl whose brother was a wealthy landowner? That she should love him, too, was too much to ask, but he dared believe that she did not dislike him.

He forced his attention back to his work. He had only known Jessica a few days—it was much too soon to dream of making her his wife.

JESSICA SETTLED DOWN after breakfast to work on the sketch of Lord Ilfracombe's hunting box. The project intrigued her. She sat for some time pondering Mr. Walsingham's—was 'elevation' what he had called it?—working out where to put the trees and the most appropriate angle for the light. The latter was not easy, as she had forgotten to ask him which direction the house would face.

It was set too square, she decided, the horizontal lines of the building parallel with the top and bottom of the sheet of paper. She would turn it a little, to give interesting lines of perspective. That, of course, gave rise to other problems as details of the façade not shown on the elevation came into view. She cast her mind back to the floor plans: did the modest portico have four pillars or only the front two? How much easier it would be if she could just pop round to Mr. Walsingham's house to ask him!

Chin in hand, she gazed out of the window at the rain falling on the river, wondering what he was doing at this moment.

This distraction did not speed her work which turned out to be more complicated than she expected anyway. She spent most of the day at it, then Nathan returned from a foray to a lending library carrying, along with a weighty volume on sheep rearing, Mr. Walsingham's floor plans.

"I got tired of your complaints," he said, "so I stopped by and picked them up for you. He needs them back, though. He's working on the heating system."

Jessica made quick copies of the parts that affected the façade and sent Tad to return the plans. To her annoyance she found that the new information necessitated a number of changes. She abandoned her pencil for the rest of the day and returned to work next morning.

By the time she and Nathan set out for the Pump Room she had produced a sketch she was not displeased with. Her brother, too, had announced his approbation.

"You and Walsingham ought to go into partnership," he teased as they walked along North Parade.

Blushing, she kept her eyes resolutely from Matthew Walsingham's front door. "It was an interesting project," she told him defensively. "Besides, I find it admirable that a gentleman who wants for nothing should take up so useful an occupation. Many in his position would simply fritter away their time in frivolous pursuits."

"True. He has mentioned that Lord Stone keeps control of the Stone Gables estate firmly in his own hands. Walsingham can hardly press for a say in the management—it would look as if he was in a hurry to inherit."

The sun peeked between passing clouds, glimmering on rain-washed paving stones, and a damp, refreshing breeze fluttered Jessica's skirts. They crossed Pierrepont Street and turned past the Abbey. As they approached the Pump Room, a young lady in a simple lavender walking dress and a straw hat with lavender ribbons emerged from the colonnade at the far end of the Pump Yard. Jessica recognized her at once but said nothing.

"By Jove," exclaimed her brother, turning his steps towards the girl and her chaperone, "isn't that Miss Pearson? Jess, you have worked a miracle."

"There is an improvement, is there not?" she said modestly.

"She's pretty as ... oh, as a picture, though that's a dashed inadequate expression. Good day, Miss Pearson. Your most obedient, ma'am." He bowed briefly to Mrs. Woodcock before turning back eagerly to her charge.

The ladies uttered polite greetings, Lucy's decidedly disjointed. Her shining eyes never left Nathan's face. Around her delicate throat she was wearing ivory beads, Jessica noted with approval, intricately carved, doubtless expensive, but suitably modest. She looked altogether charming; no wonder Nathan was dazzled.

How extraordinarily lucky if her unthinking kindness to a shy child should lead to Nathan falling in love with an heiress!

They continued into the Pump Room. Abandoned to Mrs. Woodcock's muttered platitudes, Jessica was delighted to see Matthew Walsingham standing near the door. Apparently he was watching for their arrival for he stepped forward at once, though his first words were for the chaperone.

"Good morning, Mrs. Partridge," he said blandly. "I trust I see you well?"

"Woodcock! The Honourable Mrs. Woodcock." Her name seemed to be the only thing the lady really cared about. She gave him an affronted stare and turned back to speak to Lucy.

Jessica met Matthew's sparkling grey eyes. "Wicked!" she murmured.

"Irresistible!" he responded, his voice somehow conveying a double meaning that made her drop her gaze, feeling flustered. "I want to talk to you about the drawings," he went on. "Will you allow me, at last, to take you for a drive?"

"Later, perhaps."

"That's what I thought you would say, so Hanson is bringing round the curricle in half an hour."

"I did not give you permission to read my mind, sir!" she said indignantly, then had to join in his laughter. "How dare you lead me on to make such a ridiculous statement. Oh, there is Kitty Barlow waving to us."

Mrs. Woodcock, with a glare of dislike for Mr. Walsingham, confided Lucy to Jessica's care while she went to speak to an acquaintance. The four young people went to join the Barlows' usual merry group. Jessica was glad to see that no one now looked askance at Lucy.

Maria Crane was one of the party. The pert red-head greeted Matthew with a flirtatious flicker of the lashes. "Have you taken the waters yet today, Mr. Walsingham?" she enquired archly, in a blatant attempt to ape Jessica's concern for his health.

"My cough is much improved, Miss Crane," he answered. His face was grave, but Jessica caught the amusement in his voice. "I have decided to give up drinking the stuff—on Miss Franklin's advice."

"Indeed, I gave you no such advice!" she said, startled. "You must not impute to my influence your own preference. If you are truly determined to abandon the treatment, we can only trust that you will not suffer for it."

"On the contrary, I feel better already at the very prospect of a day without the foul liquid." He turned to reply to a question from Mrs. Barlow.

His cough did indeed seem to have vanished, thought Jessica, not that it had ever been frequent. In fact, she had not heard it more than three or four times in a week. She frowned in puzzlement, but was distracted from consideration of the oddity by Kitty's request for her opinion of a new style of gathering a sleeve.

A half hour passed in chatter and strolling about the room, then Matthew drew her aside.

"I'm just going to see if Hanson is here yet with the carriage. He may not have found anyone to hold the horses or to bring a message. I shall be back in a moment."

She nodded, and he went off while she looked around for Mrs. Woodcock. "Lucy, I am leaving shortly and I must return you to your chaperone," she apologized. "I see her at the far end of the room."

"You need not go, Jess," said Nathan firmly. "I shall escort Miss Pearson."

Lucy looked up at her with sparkling eyes. "I have *so* enjoyed myself this morning. *Thank* you, Miss Franklin—Jessica." She took Nathan's arm with an almost possessive gesture.

Jessica watched them walk away, smiling at the slight spring in the girl's step. She was not at all surprised when Nathan failed to return immediately.

But so did Matthew Walsingham. He was gone at least a quarter hour, and Jessica was beginning to wonder—no, he would not desert her; something had occurred to delay him. Then she saw him crossing the room towards her.

He was tight-lipped, his expression sombre, and his limp was more pronounced than usual. When he reached her side, his smile was effortful. He made his excuses for keeping her waiting and offered his arm. "Shall we go?"

She must have looked doubtful, for he added urgently, "Please. Please come."

Unwilling to add to his unaccountable distress, she acquiesced. As they walked across the Pump Yard and under the colonnade, he congratulated her jokingly on

Lucy Pearson's transformation. By the time he handed her into the curricle she wondered whether she had imagined his previous agitation.

Taking the reins from the groom and seating himself beside her on the blue leather seat, he said, "I believe Nathan admires Miss Pearson almost as much as he admires my carriage. He was struck by it the moment he first saw it, was he not?"

"Yes, he... That is, I..." To her annoyance, Jessica felt her cheeks grow hot with remembered embarrassment. "It is an exceptionally elegant vehicle," she said, self-consciously but firmly, "and your bays are splendid."

"Are they not?" he agreed, setting them in motion. "I had a notion, that day, that they had caught your eye."

"Oh!" Her exclamation was stifled, but attempting to sound unconcerned she enquired cautiously, "That day?"

"Your first in Bath, was it? The first time I saw you."

"Then you *did* recognize me! And you are laughing at me. You must have thought me shockingly bold, to be staring so at a stranger."

"On the contrary, I was sure you had turned to speak to your brother, and I wished I had had the good fortune to capture your attention as I had his."

"You are kind, sir. I did hope you had not noticed me in that sadly dowdy bonnet. It was the best one in Durham but disgracefully provincial, I fear. Besides, I had no heart for shopping while Nathan was in America." When he did not respond she glanced sideways at him, to find the teasing look gone. There was a heavy frown between his brows, and his eyes were troubled. "What is it? Have I said something to distress you?"

"No, of course not. It is nothing."

"Are you in pain, Mr. Walsingham? Shall we go home? Pray tell me what is the matter."

He was silent for a moment, guiding his horses into the Lansdown Road, then he burst out, his tone anguished, "That battle—they're calling it Waterloo. Hanson had the latest newspaper. Oh, we beat the Frenchies all right, but 'fore God, it was a Pyrrhic victory. Twenty thousand dead on our side, they say. The Highland Brigade cut to pieces, and Kempt's and the King's German Legion. Picton gone, and half the Duke's staff, and God knows who else."

"Your friends..." Her heart ached for his sorrow.

"...Those few left after the Peninsula. I don't know—the lists are not published yet. War is Hell, Jessica. Never let anyone tell you it's glorious. But this is no fitting subject for a fine day and a lovely lady." With a visible effort he pulled himself together. "I suppose you have not yet had time to begin the drawing you promised me?"

Bemused by his unthinking use of her Christian name, she was glad to help divert his mind from destruction to creation. "For Lord Ilfracombe? I have finished it, to the best of my abilities. I never thought it could be so difficult to work out where a shadow ought to lie. You must look at it and judge whether it is sufficiently accurate."

"I have no doubt of it, as long as you have resisted the temptation to embellish my façade with angels on ladders. I sketched in a heating system yesterday. It will take some research to design it properly, but I want to make sure Ilfracombe is still interested before I do the work. He may have found another architect by now."

"You said he is your friend."

"He is, though he is considerably older than I. He was a protégé of my father at the Home Office, and after my father's death I used to spend part of my school holidays with him."

"He is still a bachelor, I suppose?"

Matthew laughed. "You are thinking of the lack of a drawing room. Yes, he is a bachelor, though he's titled, wealthy, generally considered handsome, and popular with the ladies."

"A very paragon! Perhaps he is unable to choose among all those vying for his favour."

"Perhaps, but rumour has it that he suffered a disappointment in youth. I did hope once that he and my aunt Caroline—but nothing came of it, and after all I was a mere child. Doubtless I misunderstood the situation, or perhaps it was wishful thinking. Aunt Caroline came to live with my father and me when my mother, her older sister, died, and of course Lord Ilfracombe often visited my father."

They had reached the top of Lansdown Hill. He turned off the road onto a grassy track, and drew his team to a halt facing back across the town and the river to Beechen Cliff. The well-bred bays stood quietly, with an occasional toss of the head. Jessica duly admired the view, but she was far more interested in Mr. Walsingham's family history.

"Where did you spend the rest of your school holidays?" she asked, "when you were not with Lord Ilfracombe? Oh dear, that sounds shockingly inquisitive."

He grinned at her. "It is, but I am by far too good-natured to leave your unpardonable curiosity unsatisfied. From the age of thirteen I made my home at Stone Gables, with my mother's brother, Uncle Horace—he of the bilious rebellion against Bath's waters—and Aunt Caroline.''

"Who must be his sister, then. She never married?"

"No. I cannot imagine why not, for she is pretty even now, and amiable, and imbued with all the domestic virtues, yet not at all stuffy. I'm very fond of Aunt Caroline. And before you ask—for I see the question hovering on your lips—my mother had one other sister, who is married. There are also a number of aunts and uncles on my father's side of the family, and hordes of cousins.'' He grimaced as if at an unpleasant memory. "Some of my relatives I'm happy not to see from one year's end to the next. Now it's your turn."

"I have hordes of cousins, too, of varying degrees. In fact, Aunt Tibby is not really my aunt, and I couldn't explain the precise relationship if I tried." That had the merit of being true, if misleading. "I do have real aunts and uncles, all of whom wanted me to go and live with them when Papa died two years ago, as Nathan was already in America. I would not leave Langdale, though. There have been Franklins at Langdale for two centuries." And that also was true but misleading, Jessica thought, since the Franklins had never actually owned a square inch of land. Enough of family histories! "Do you go to the concert at the Octagon Chapel tonight, sir?"

"If I may accompany you," he said with flattering promptness, then a sombre shadow crossed his face. "Did you know that the programme has been changed? In celebration of the victory at Waterloo, they are to perform the 'Te Deum' and 'Jubilate' that Handel wrote for the Peace of Utrecht. A famous irony, is it not? A century has passed and yet again we have been fighting France."

Jessica put her hand over his. "I shall understand if you decide not to go," she said softly.

His hand turned under hers, clasped and pressed it, and he looked down at her with a crooked smile. "I'll be there. Music is not to be blamed for man's madness—unless it be the music of bagpipes." He laughed, in real amusement with a bitter undertone. "Oh, that was a splendid charge the Highlanders made."

The horses were growing restless. With casual expertise he turned the curricle and drove back down the hill.

Tad must have been watching for his mistress's return, for hardly had the carriage stopped before Number 15 when he was racing out to hand Jessica down. She thanked him with a smile and turned back to Mr. Walsingham.

"You'll want to send the papers to Lord Ilfracombe at once, will you not? Tad shall bring you my little contribution."

"Thank you, Miss Franklin. You're right, the sooner the better. I'll see you this evening." He saluted with his whip.

As she crossed the stone bridge over the area to the front door, Jessica heard no sound of hooves or wheels. Was he sitting there watching her? She willed herself not to look back, but in the end could not resist the temptation.

He was laughing at her again! She wrinkled her nose at him and stepped into the house.

"Jessica!" Nathan burst out of the drawing room, followed by Aunt Tibby. "How could you!"

"How could I what?" she asked blankly.

"Go off with him without even a groom for propriety! I met his Hanson on the way home."

"Indeed, Jessica, it is not at all the thing to be jaunting about alone with a gentleman. We must hope that no one saw you, or I fear you will be called fast, which could ruin your prospects."

Dismayed, Jessica sank onto the straight chair by the hall table. "Oh dear, I never even thought how it would look. You may not believe me, but it never crossed my mind. Sometimes I feel as if I've known Matthew . . ."

"Matthew!" Nathan exclaimed.

". . .Mr. Walsingham forever. He did not attempt any familiarities, I promise you. I'm sure he would not dream of taking advantage of my indiscretion."

"It must have been he who dismissed the groom," her brother pointed out with inexorable logic.

"He did not do it from any dishonourable motive. He had just read a newspaper and his mind was on other matters," Jessica defended him. Suddenly she wondered whether talking to Nathan about Waterloo might help Matthew, and whether learning of the dreadful slaughter from Matthew rather than a newspaper might be best for her brother. He did not appear to have heard the news. She knew that many of his fellow-soldiers from America had gone to Belgium on their return to Europe.

With renewed energy she jumped up and took from the hall table the roll of paper with her drawing of Lord Ilfracombe's hunting box. "Be a dear and take this round to Mr. Walsingham," she said, handing it to Nathan. "He's waiting for it, and I believe he wants a word with you."

Reduced at a stroke from stern head of the family to messenger, Nathan cast her a resentful glance but complied.

"All very well," said Miss Tibbett, reverting to their original subject as the door closed behind him, "but Mr. Walsingham's honour is not in question. It is your lack of discretion that will shock the tattlers."

Jessica kissed her. "I'm sorry, Tibby dear, I shan't do anything so shatterbrained again. We must just hope that no one noticed us." She went slowly upstairs to take off her bonnet.

Mr. Walsingham's honour was not in question. She trusted him. Today she had seen a deeply serious side to the amusing, frivolous gentleman, and respect had been added to her liking.

She stood by her chamber window, swinging her bonnet by the ribbons and gazing out unseeing at the Avon's rushing waters. Was she falling in love? What incredible luck that so remarkably attractive a gentleman should be heir to the wealthy Viscount Stone of Stone Gables! Yes, she rather thought she was on the brink of falling in love, and she suspected that he was far from indifferent to her.

CHAPTER TEN

"HERE'S YOUR HOT WATER, Miss Jessica." Sukey flung back the curtains to reveal a cloudless sky.

Jessica yawned and stretched luxuriously. Memory flooded back. Last night Matthew had sat beside her at the concert and she had known him as moved as she was by Handel's stirring music. And he had already engaged her for the first dance at the Lower Rooms tonight.

She became aware that the maid was standing with hands on hips, regarding her with an odd look. "Thank you, Sukey. It's going to be a glorious day."

"That's as may be, miss, and I'm sure I'll be downright sorry to spoil it for you, but there's that you ought to know."

Too happy to be alarmed, she smiled and asked, "What's the matter?"

"Our Tad were down to t'Pig and Whistle last night," the maid said in an ominous voice.

"He's entitled to his pint of ale, Sukey. Don't tell me he overindulged in Blue Ruin."

"Oh no, miss, he's not one for tippling gin and he don't like brandy above half, neither. It's who he met's t'trouble."

"You are afraid he is getting into bad company?"

"Not *him*. He run across a groom from Stone Gables, come to Bath on an errand for his lordship. Seems as how the viscount's got another nevvie staying wi' him, a Mr. Archibald Biggin if Tad recalled t'name aright. And seems as how Lord Stone and Mr. Walsingham had a right set-to a fortnight since. And seems as how his lordship up and sent for his lawyer to change his will.''

Jessica sat bolt upright. "No! Really, Sukey, you should have more sense than to believe tavern gossip. I'm sure Tad completely misunderstood the case. I daresay he did have a glass too many of gin and he's mixing up a story about someone quite different."

"He didn't act fuddled, miss, when he come home, and I've never knowed him go on the mop, nor Mrs. Ancaster hasn't neither."

"He has been spreading this wicked tale? I will not have it!"

"He wouldn't tell no one outside t'house, nor wouldn't any of us, Miss Jessica." Sukey sounded injured.

"Nor will you tell Sir Nathan, I trust. He would be shocked to think his servants are no better than scandalmongers."

"I just thought as you ought to know."

"Well I don't believe a word of it. I hope you have something better to do with your time than to stand there slandering your betters."

The maid marched out, muttering audibly, "There's none so blind as them that won't see."

Jessica sank back against her pillows. Matthew a fraud? It could not be true. Perhaps he had indeed quarrelled with his uncle—no doubt the viscount's bilious attacks made him testy. An argument together with the visit of another nephew would be enough to start rumours of a changed will, particularly if the lawyer happened to visit at the same time. But the lawyer might have been called in for any number of reasons, and more than likely Mr. Archibald Biggin often stayed with his uncle.

Doubtless the groom had embellished the story to make himself interesting, and Tad had confused the details, and Sukey had misreported the whole business.

All the same, Jessica felt she had been unnecessarily harsh with the maid, who was only trying to aid her mistress. She would apologize and buy her some ribbons. She and Nathan were lucky to have such loyal servants, for without their backing this venture would have been impossible; lucky also that Langdale was too far off for casual rumour to give them away.

Matthew Walsingham's valet and groom must be equally dedicated to his service, but Stone Gables was too close for safety.

Without enthusiasm she climbed out of bed, washed in the now tepid water, and put on a gown of the thinnest India muslin. It was going to be a long, hot day. Her seamstress was expecting her for a fitting, and then she was to meet Lucy to go shopping. Somehow the elegant shops of Milsom Street failed to attract her this morning.

The shopping expedition was not a success. Lucy wilted in the heat reflecting from the pale Bath-stone walls and pavement. They took refuge in a circulating library, only to be driven thence by the arrival of the rakish Lord Alsop. Jessica summoned a chair for Lucy and walked beside it the short but uphill distance to the Circus. When they reached the Pearsons' house, she was very glad to accept a glass of lemonade and renew her acquaintance with Mr. Pearson.

"I'm that grateful to you, ma'am, for taking our Lucy under your wing," he said. "I was in a fair way to leaving Bath in despair before, for she wasn't enjoying herself though she tried to gammon her old pa she was." He shook his head fondly at his daughter.

Jessica liked the bluff, shrewd man who so obviously adored his only child. Nonetheless, as she was driven home in the blue and gold barouche, she hoped Nathan would be well and truly caught before he discovered that his beloved's papa was a Cit.

Rumour was a chancy thing. Word of Mr. Pearson's occupation had not yet reached her brother's ears, yet Matthew Walsingham had been unmasked by a chance meeting in a tavern.

Since she had lost her mother at the age of twelve, Jessica had always turned to Tibby when troubled. Arriving at home, she was glad to find her former governess alone in the back parlour, perusing Caesar's *Commentarii de bello Gallico* (the section on the invasion of Britain), which she regarded as light reading.

"*'Exigua parte aestatis reliqua,'*" Jessica quoted. "That's the only bit I remember, I fear."

"Alas, your father did not approve of a female studying Latin." Miss Tibbett lowered her book and peered over her spectacles. "Something is troubling you, my dear." She pushed her spectacles up to a precarious perch on her head as Jessica sank into a chair.

"It's so very dreadful, Tibby, and I don't know what to believe." She explained what Sukey had told her.

"What is so very dreadful?" Miss Tibbett enquired with interest.

"I *like* him. I trusted him."

"If it is true, you are in no position to throw stones," Miss Tibbett pointed out. "But it seems unlikely that he should be living in Lord Stone's house if they have quarrelled irrevocably."

"That's a good point." Jessica brightened, then frowned. "On the other hand, there is the business of his cough. He told me he was in Bath to take the waters for his cough, yet he only coughed three or four times in my presence, and I only saw him drink the waters once. I believe he invented the whole as an explanation for his presence here, especially as he now claims to be cured yet he does not leave Bath."

"I do not find that hard to understand."

"You mean he stays because he likes me?" she said wistfully. "I like him, too, and that is the trouble. If he is not wealthy after all, how can I marry him?"

"Has he asked you?" Tibby looked dismayed.

"No, and if he did I should have to tell him that I am not wealthy, either, and he would cry off."

"Not necessarily, not if Tad's tale is erroneous, which it may well be. I think you are making mountains out of molehills, my dear. You are not committed to Mr. Walsingham, and much as you like him you must not confine your efforts to him. There are, after all, other..."

"...Fish in the sea. Yes, of course you are right. After all, I've only known the wretched man a fortnight, so why should I care?" Jessica heaved a deep sigh. "There may be others whom I could like just as well—since I met him I have not even looked about me. I shall begin tonight, at the Lower Rooms."

Miss Tibbett nodded her approval and reached up for her spectacles to resume her reading. Jessica spent the next five minutes disentangling the wretched things from her hair.

Jessica had no intention of attracting unwelcome comment by so drastic an act as refusing to stand up with Matthew Walsingham at that evening's assembly. Doing her best to treat him as a mere acquaintance, though a pleasant one, she realized to what extent she had fallen into intimacy with him. She was glad that the country dance allowed little opportunity for conversation.

Nonetheless, he seemed to notice an alteration in her demeanour, for he gave her a puzzled look as he escorted her to where Miss Tibbett sat with Mrs. Barlow. Then his face cleared.

"It is wretchedly hot in here this evening," he said cheerfully, taking her fan from her as she sat down and wielding it with such vigour that her ringlets bobbed. "Perhaps you would like to take a turn out in the fresh air, Miss Franklin?"

"Oh no, I think..." Uncertain what to say, Jessica glanced towards the nearby French windows that stood open to the narrow terrace running the length of the ballroom. Not even the fussiest of dowagers could complain of a draught tonight. What she saw made her spring to her feet. "Lucy... Lord Alsop... Oh, yes, let us go at once. Where is Nathan?"

The baron, gripping Lucy's upper arm, was urging her towards the open doors. As Jessica approached, Matthew close behind her, the girl glanced back with a desperate look. They reached her just as Nathan appeared on Lord Alsop's other side, his face dark with fury.

"My lord," said Jessica quickly with an artificial titter, "I do believe you have quite forgot you asked me for the next dance."

Before the nonplussed gentleman could respond, or her brother could explode, Matthew put in, "And I fear, Miss Pearson, that you have done the same for me.

What is worse, by the way Sir Nathan is glaring at me I suspect you promised to stand up with him, too. Pistols at dawn, Nathan?''

Lord Alsop blenched and swallowed his protest. Jessica took him by the sleeve and practically dragged him to join a set that was just forming. She looked back to see Lucy gazing up with worship in her eyes at Nathan, who grinned at Matthew, offered the girl his arm, and proceeded with her towards the terrace.

''The heat made Miss Pearson feel faint,'' said the baron smoothly. ''A delicate girl—it seemed best to take her into the fresh air without waiting for her next partner to find us. How delightfully you look this evening, Miss Franklin. Quite the most elegant young lady in the room.'' His cold eyes assessed her aquamarines.

Jessica, who was rather pleased with the way the new green velvet ribbons had refurbished her sprig muslin, fluttered her eyelashes after the style of Maria Crane and murmured, ''You are too kind, my lord. It is gratifying to have as my partner the most stylish gentleman present.''

The lines of dissipation on his face settled into an expression of self-satisfaction. ''Nugee makes my coats,'' he told her complacently. ''There are those who swear by Weston, but to my way of thinking his designs lack that little something.''

The little something, Jessica assumed, comprised the wasp waist, shoulder pads, wide lapels and huge gilt buttons. Nor did the fact that the coat was made of violet satin reconcile her to it. She wondered whether Lucy's colourful gowns had originally drawn the fop to her—but no, undoubtedly the attraction had been her jewellery.

She realized his lordship's eyes had moved down from her necklace to her bosom, and they were no longer cold or smug. To her relief, at that moment Matthew joined the set with Kitty Barlow and the music started.

At the end of the dance, Jessica was forced to promise Lord Alsop another, later in the evening. She declined a stroll on the terrace, however, grateful for Nathan's prompt appearance at her side.

"My turn, Jess," he said.

She looked around in dismay. "Where is Lucy? Has Mr. Walsingham gone to her?"

"I persuaded Mrs. Woodcock to take her home. Your new admirer was right about one thing, the heat really made her feel unwell."

"New admirer! Do not say so!"

He laughed, but said seriously, "I shall have to keep an eye on the man. You can take care of yourself, I know, but Lucy is such a timid little innocent."

Though she knew he meant to compliment her, Jessica was a little put out by her brother's comment. If timid innocence elicited such devotion, perhaps her own independent spirit was less desirable than she had thought.

Following Tibby's advice, she avoided dancing again with Matthew. However, the gentlemen who stood up with her were known to have not a feather to fly with or at best, like Mr. Barlow and Lord Peter Glossop, to be possessed of a competence insufficient to purchase an expensive lease as a bride-gift. Matthew, meanwhile, took to the floor with Maria Crane and Annabel Forrester in turn, neither of whom, Jessica guessed, had heard rumours of his insolvency.

In Lucy's absence, Nathan was also pursued by young ladies of slender means. The whole of Bath Society seemed convinced that the Franklins were decidedly plump in the pocket.

That was just what Jessica had wanted, of course. Somehow it had not dawned on her that as well as attracting eligible gentlemen, her supposed wealth would bring a swarm of acknowledged fortune hunters. In a mood of dissatisfaction, she moved on Lord Peter's arm towards the chaperones.

From the corner of her eye she saw Lord Alsop approaching and realised it was time for her second dance with him.

"Aunt Tibby, I'm afraid this shocking heat does not agree with you," she said swiftly.

"I do have a bit of a headache," that lady admitted. No one could accuse her of being slow on the uptake.

"We must take you home at once, dear Aunt. Here is Nathan, he shall call for a chair."

Mrs. Barlow intervened. "There's no need for you to miss the dancing, Miss Franklin. I'll be happy to chaperone you and I daresay Sir Nathan won't mind coming back for you."

"I fear Jessica's tisane is the *only* remedy for one of my headaches." Miss Tibbett pronounced this inspired invention in failing tones.

Lord Alsop was forced to accept Jessica's excuses with a good grace. Five minutes later she and Miss Tibbett were ensconced in chairs with Nathan walking homeward between them.

"My apologies for tearing you away early, Aunt Tibby," Jessica teased, "but I could not face dancing with that man again."

"I was quite ready to leave. Mrs. Barlow is a sadly ignorant woman, though good-hearted."

"Sufficiently wide-awake to see through your play-acting," Nathan told her, "but kind enough, I trust, not to give you away even though I was engaged to Kitty Barlow for the last dance." He fell silent then, and did not speak again until the front door of Number 15 closed behind them. "It's this damnable plot of yours, Jess," he burst out then. "All these girls are setting their caps at me because they think I'm rich."

"I'm sorry," she said guiltily, "but you cannot very well go around denying it."

"I know. A proper nodcock I should look, and I daresay no one would believe me anyway."

"Lucy doesn't care if you're rich," Jessica pointed out.

"No, but that's equally damnable, because when she finds out I'm not she'll think I only care because she is!"

In an atmosphere of gloom they all went up to bed.

CHAPTER ELEVEN

MATTHEW GAZED OUT gloomily at the grey drizzle. It had been raining now for four days, postponing the boating expedition on the canal and curtailing all other social activities. As a near neighbour and a friend of Nathan's, he had taken the liberty of calling at Number 15 more often than might otherwise have been proper, only to be made aware of a definite reserve in Jessica's manner. He was at a loss to account for it, unless her aunt had warned her that she was being too familiar.

It was hard to believe he had known her less than a month. Already his servants had reported gossip linking them as a couple, which might have offended Jessica, he realized, if word had reached her ears.

The newspaper he had been reading rustled as he shifted restlessly. The constant dampness made his leg ache. Perhaps exercise might help, he thought, and he was rising from his chair by the fire when his valet came in.

"There's a messenger from Lord Ilfracombe, sir. His lordship's just arrived at the York House Hotel and hopes you will dine with him tonight."

"Tell him I'll be there in half an hour." Matthew cheered up at once. It was only six o'clock, but the earl, though a gentleman of conventional habits, was a close enough friend not to mind if he arrived early. He changed quickly and strode out into the rain, scarcely noticing it now in his eagerness to discover Ilfracombe's opinion of his plans for the Leicestershire hunting box.

Though travelling alone, the earl had taken a spacious suite of rooms on the first floor of the hotel. In this case "alone" meant accompanied only by his secretary, valet, footman, groom, and coachman, as befitted a member of the government and a wealthy landowner. Matthew was admitted by the footman and found his lordship already contemplating the drawings, spread on the table in the dining parlour. He looked round with a smile.

"I like it, Matthew."

"Do you, sir?" Matthew grinned, more pleased than he could say. "I'm glad to hear you say so."

"You have caught the feeling of informality I desire, unlike the other fellow who showed me his design. This sketch of the front expresses it best." He indicated Jessica's drawing. "I'm also particularly impressed by your heating system. There are one or two minor changes I want to discuss. Have a glass of madeira, and let us talk about it."

The secretary, a discreet young man, poured a glass of wine and gave it to Matthew, then sat down at the table to take notes. By the time the papers had to be cleared to allow the hotel waiters to set the table for dinner, they had settled on the alterations to be made.

"I'll have everything ready for you in a day or two," Matthew promised the earl, rolling up the plans. "Are you staying in Bath?"

"Yes, I shall stay a few days. I'm not in any great hurry and I have not visited the place in twenty years." His lordship looked a trifle self-conscious, Matthew noted with surprise, but he forgot the matter as they sat down to dinner.

The secretary dined with them. Over a succulent sirloin with new peas and asparagus, the gentlemen discussed Wellington's victory at Waterloo and what was to be done with the fugitive ex-Emperor of the French. Claret flowed freely. When the table was cleared the secretary took himself off to write some letters. Matthew accepted a glass of port, then set it down after one sip. Now that they were private he wanted to discuss his situation with Lord Ilfracombe, but he was not sure how to introduce the subject. Gazing into the rich, tawny depths of the wine, he wished for inspiration.

"How is it you have taken up architecture again?" asked his lordship helpfully. "I thought it a mere pastime while you were convalescent."

"So it was, but everything has changed. My uncle has disowned me."

"Lord Stone? Devil take it, Matthew, he's been a second father to you these dozen years. What have you done to turn him against you?"

Matthew took a fortifying gulp of port. "You may have heard about a certain race down St. James's Street?"

"With your ladybird in a wheelbarrow?" Ilfracombe grinned. "Yes, and I wished I'd been there. It was a nine hours' wonder in the clubs, as I'm sure you are aware. Liverpool nearly fell into an apoplexy trying not to laugh. Don't tell me Stone took such a lark amiss? I had not thought him so straitlaced."

"I daresay he might have thought the whole thing a good joke had the news not arrived when he was laid up with an attack of dyspepsia. As it is, he took exception not so much to my want of propriety as to my having wagered a couple of hundred on the outcome.''

"I understood you won."

"I did," Matthew confirmed glumly. "Uncle Horace considers that to risk so much on so uncertain an outcome shows that I have no notion of the value of money. So to teach me a permanent lesson he has changed his will in favour of Cousin Archibald."

"Archibald Biggin, the canting evangelical? Good gad! I thought he couldn't stomach the fellow."

"He never could, but I suppose the dyspepsia has altered the condition of his stomach." His *bon mot* failed to cheer him. "The result is that I am altogether cut out of his will. You were one of my trustees; you know how my father left me. There's enough to live on, just, but I hope to supplement my income by taking up architecture seriously."

"An excellent notion." Lord Ilfracombe nodded and refilled Matthew's glass, which he had emptied without noticing. "I shall naturally recommend you to all of my acquaintance. However, I daresay it will take some time to develop a following. Of course I shall pay you at once for your work, but if there is anything else I can do for you in the meantime, you must not hesitate to ask."

"If Uncle Horace has been a father to me, you have been a favourite uncle," said Matthew gratefully. "I am hopeful, though, that my other scheme will soon come to fruition." He frowned, thinking of Jessica's recent coolness. "There do seem to be some unexpected complications."

"You have a second string to your bow? That's wise. What is your other scheme?"

"To marry a rich bride. Aunt Caroline suggested it."

"I refuse to believe that Miss Stone advised you to become a fortune hunter!" The earl sounded furious.

"Well, not precisely. She was joking. She did not intend that I should set out deliberately to woo an heiress."

"But that is what you have done? Caroline always was wont to see the best in people, and you were always her darling. She was scarce out of the schoolroom when your mother died and she took her place," he added with a hint of bitterness.

Ignoring his irrelevance, Matthew hastened to dispute his lordship's conclusion. "I don't mean to marry only for money, I promise you. But it was convenient to come to Bath, and there was no harm in hoping that I might meet a pleasant young lady who happened to be wealthy. And I have!" he exulted. "Jessica Franklin is beautiful and witty and altogether enchanting, and her brother owns vast estates in the North, and..."

"And she knows your circumstances and loves you in spite of them?"

"Well, no. You could hardly expect me to go trumpeting around Bath that I'm no longer Viscount Stone's heir. Of course I shall tell her before I ask her to marry me."

"Thus breaking the girl's heart, perhaps, when she realizes you courted her for her money. I did not think you capable of such deceit."

Matthew took another draught of port to drown his guilt. "You don't understand. I'm in love with Jessica, heels over head, and I know she likes me. But if she finds out now," he said desperately, "before I can fix her affection..."

"Don't worry, I shan't give you away—for the present." There was deep disapprobation in his lordship's tone. He hesitated, brow wrinkled in thought. "I believe it will be best if I remain in Bath for a while to keep an eye on the situation. I shall do what I can for you, Matthew, but I warn you, if I decide that this young woman is in danger of being hurt, I shall not hesitate to act."

"Thank you, sir. I would not hurt her for the world—" he dropped his head into his hands "—but I realize I am not in any position to make you believe that!"

"WHO IS THAT distinguished-looking gentleman with Mr. Walsingham?" asked Kitty Barlow.

"I haven't the least notion," said Jessica sharply. She did not care for the implication that any companion of Matthew Walsingham's must be known to her. However, she could not resist following Kitty's gaze with a quick glance. The Pump Room was crowded on the first fine morning after days of rain, yet she picked out Matthew's tall figure instantly.

"That's Ilfracombe," Lord Peter answered Kitty's query. Such unwonted volubility was becoming commonplace in Miss Barlow's undemanding presence and Jessica scented a match.

At present she was more interested in Lord Ilfracombe. As an old family friend he must surely know the truth about Matthew's position. She wished she could just ask outright and set her doubts to rest. That course being unthinkable, she contented herself with favouring him with a sunny smile when Matthew introduced him.

"How do you do, my lord. May one hope that your arrival in Bath indicates your interest in Mr. Walsingham's designs for your hunting box?"

He looked amused at her bluntness, his searching expression lightened by a smile. He was attractive, she thought, not tall but strongly built, his figure that of a younger man than the steel-grey at his temples and the lightly etched lines in his face proclaimed. In his mid-forties, perhaps; that would fit in with what Matthew had told her of him.

"I am more than interested, Miss Franklin," he replied. "I have every intention of using Matthew's plans. I understand the sketch that proved the deciding factor was of your workmanship?"

"My drawing influenced you in his favour?" Delighted, Jessica beamed at Matthew. His answering smile seemed oddly relieved.

"It did, ma'am. Being inexpert in reading plans, I could not have pictured the building without it. You are talented."

"Thank you, sir. I have never attempted such a thing before, though, as I told Ma—Mr. Walsingham, I like to draw buildings because they do not move."

Lord Ilfracombe laughed. She decided she liked him and happily introduced him to Nathan and Lucy, who came up at that moment. Lucy was struck dumb, but the earl stood chatting to Nathan while Jessica satisfied Kitty's curiosity about her drawing of the hunting box.

Bob Barlow arrived with Maria Crane and Annabel Forrester. Miss Crane promptly turned her fluttering eyelashes on Lord Ilfracombe. He parried her coquetries with amused indulgence. However, when the subject of that evening's assembly in the Upper Rooms arose, it was to Jessica that his lordship first turned with a request for a dance. Flattered, she accepted with alacrity.

Now why, she wondered, should Matthew cast his friend a glance both reproachful and dismayed? He must have noticed her coolness this past week—that would explain also his relief when she showed an interest in the success of his building designs. She did not want to hurt him, and she certainly had no intention of refusing to stand up with him, as he quickly requested. Of course, she also promised dances to Mr. Barlow, Lord Peter, and Nathan.

On the other hand, Matthew went on to engage Kitty, Maria, Annabel and Lucy to dance with him, so perhaps he was not so cast down at Jessica's aloofness as she hoped.

Bother the man! He had her so confused she didn't know what to hope for!

When she saw Lord Alsop approaching, though, she had no doubt of her feelings: relief that she was already engaged for every set at the assembly. The baron's cold eyes were on Lucy, and Jessica saw that Nathan was at that moment speaking to Miss Forrester. She moved towards her friend.

Lord Alsop bowed. "Miss Pearson, may I beg the pleasure of standing up with you at the Upper Rooms tonight?"

"Oh, my lord, I...I'm not sure...." Lucy stammered in her soft, shy voice.

"Your card is full, is it not, Lucy?" Jessica interrupted. "I fear, my lord, you are too late."

He was not so easily deterred. "Are you quite certain, Miss Pearson, that you have not a single set free?"

Since Lucy was obviously not at all certain, Jessica was relieved when Nathan swung round, realizing at last that something was amiss.

"Miss Pearson is engaged for the entire evening, sir," he said, his voice cool but civil. "I have kept a count for her since she has not her card with her."

The baron cast him a look of venomous dislike, but Jessica saw that Nathan was aware only of the fervent gratitude in Lucy's brown eyes. The momentary silence among the four of them was broken by Maria Crane's invitation:

"Mama says that if the weather is still warm tomorrow we shall have our sketching picnic at Beechen Cliff at last. I do hope you will all come."

Kitty Barlow accepted with instant enthusiasm. "Oh, yes, I am sure Mama will let me go, do you not think so, Bob?"

"We are to have a contest for the ladies," Maria explained to Lord Ilfracombe. "Will you be judge of who draws the best perspective of Bath, my lord?"

"By all means, ma'am," the earl agreed. Jessica heard him mutter to Matthew, "If I cannot contrive to please all parties, I don't deserve my seat in the Lords!"

"Rather you than me," Matthew murmured, laughing. He turned to Jessica. "Do you go, Miss Franklin?"

"Yes, we shall go, shall we not, Nathan?" She was ridiculously pleased that Matthew had asked her before accepting the invitation on his own behalf. "Lucy, I'll go with you to ask Mrs. Woodcock."

As she and Lucy moved away, she heard Lord Alsop's smug voice, "I shall be delighted to join you, Miss Crane. Pray allow me to put my carriage at your disposal."

Lucy clutched Jessica's arm. "If he is to go, I do not care to," she whispered.

Jessica sighed. "Maria cannot have noticed that he was with us when she issued her invitation, and then it was too late to withdraw it. I am sure she dislikes the wretched man as much as we do. You cannot always avoid him though, Lucy. Do come to the picnic. Nathan will be sadly disappointed if you don't, as shall I, and between us we shall protect you from Lord Alsop's horrid wiles."

"I always feel quite safe with Sir Nathan," Lucy admitted. "He is so very kind and he always knows just what to say. I was afraid I should have to dance with Lord Alsop tonight."

"That's the trouble with the public assemblies in Bath as opposed to the private balls in London." Jessica recalled that her companion had failed to gain entrée to the exclusive Society of London. "I mean, there are so many entertainments there that one could simply avoid a party where one knew someone unpleasant was going to be, without giving up parties altogether."

"I should not mind giving up parties. I prefer a quiet evening at home, just family or a few close friends. How delightful it must be to live at Langdale, where your nearest neighbours are miles away."

"Well, yes, I love Langdale, of course. But I must confess I thoroughly enjoy dancing and concerts and plays, too. I am very glad we came to Bath."

"Oh, so am I," cried Lucy. "Otherwise I should never have met you . . . nor Sir Nathan."

And that, agreed Jessica silently, would have been a great pity. If only Nathan fell deep enough in love with Lucy to ignore the fact that her father was in trade—and to dismiss his scruples about fortune-hunting!

CHAPTER TWELVE

"I WARNED YOU." Laughing, Jessica looked up at Lord Ilfracombe. "The foreground is acceptably rendered, and the nearer part of the town most accurately detailed, but where everything begins to merge with distance I simply cannot do it justice."

"If nothing else, you win the prize for honesty, Miss Franklin." He sighed. "I daresay I ought to take a look at the other young ladies' efforts."

"Certainly you must." She was flattered by the earl's unwillingness to leave her side. He had singled her out from the start of the expedition up Beechen Cliff, to the evident annoyance of Maria Crane and Annabel Forrester. And last night, at the assembly, he had vanished into the card room after a single dance with her.

"My lord!" Maria's patience was at an end. He rose politely from his seat on the bench as she approached, sketch book at the ready. "Here is my drawing for your appraisal."

Jessica also stood up, turning away from the view of the town to look back to where Mrs. Crane's picnic was set out invitingly in the shade of the beech trees, with the chaperones already seated at a folding table. As she started towards the array of rugs and hampers, Matthew came to meet her.

"I am judged and found wanting," she told him.

"He hasn't seen the others yet. Let me see." He took her sketch book and found the place. "Hmm, I daresay one could put a name to every street and a number to every house in the middle ground. But why have you drawn clouds in the sky? For once there's none to be seen."

"Those are hills, not clouds. Look, there are trees growing on them."

"Oh, I thought those were birds." He grinned at her. "You take the first prize for architectural excellence, though. Come and have some cherries."

"I need something more substantial than that. Drawing birds and clouds is hard work." She seated herself on a cushion and arranged her skirts.

"I'll bring you some cold chicken and veal and ham pie. Lemonade or cider?"

"Lemonade, if you please, kind sir."

While he was filling a plate for her, Jessica was joined by Nathan and Lucy, and then Lord Ilfracombe sat down on her other side.

"Who won, my lord?" she enquired.

"Miss Crane for superior perspective, Miss Barlow for shading, Miss Forrester for... hmm, let me see."

Jessica laughed. "I can see that your talents must be most useful to the government, sir."

Matthew returned, accompanied by a hired waiter bearing a tray who took orders from the others.

"Have I taken your place, Walsingham?" Lord Ilfracombe asked blandly, but he made no effort to move.

Matthew, looking vexed, was forced to find a seat at some little distance, where Annabel Forrester, Kitty Barlow, and Lord Peter soon joined him. Though she enjoyed the earl's company, Jessica could not help glancing their way now and then. Mr. Walsingham appeared to be quickly consoled for his vexation, for Annabel's giggle and Kitty's merry laugh rang out often, and even Lord Peter was heard to utter a snort of amusement.

The waiter made the rounds with a basket of cherries and Jessica helped herself to a handful. The scarlet fruits were crisp and sweet, the crimson richly juicy. She heard Kitty counting cherry stones: "Tinker, tailor, soldier, sailor..." and her squeal of dismay as she ended on "beggarman."

"Waiter, some more cherries for Miss Barlow," called Matthew.

"Count yours, Miss Franklin," Lord Ilfracombe suggested with a smile.

"I am not superstitious," she told him, but surreptitiously, under her breath, she was doing just that. Rich man—no, there was another by the chicken bone; poor man—surely she had eaten more than that. Ah, there were five more hidden under the pile of stems. Beggarman, thief, tinker, tailor, soldier... Soldier!

The waiter came by collecting plates and she quickly handed him hers. She was not in the least superstitious. She was going to marry a rich man, not a soldier.

Bob Barlow was demonstrating to Maria Crane how to start with the end of a cherry stem between one's lips and gobble one's way up it until the fruit ended in one's mouth. He neatly turned it with his tongue and out popped the stem. Kitty took off her hat and hung pairs of cherries over her ears for earrings. Thus inspired, Nathan showed Lucy how to squeeze a stone between one's fingers and make it shoot away several feet. Entering into the spirit, Matthew suggested a contest between the gentlemen to see who could fire a cherry stone the farthest.

Lord Ilfracombe rose to his feet with a groan. "I believe I am growing too old for picnics," he said to Jessica, offering his hands to help her rise. "I ought to have sat at the table with the chaperones. Do you care to stroll a little farther along the path?"

"That would be pleasant. I'll just tell my aunt where I am going."

She went over to the folding table Mrs. Crane had provided for herself, Mrs. Woodcock, and Miss Tibbett. Lord Alsop had taken his luncheon there, having apparently decided that dignity and comfort were more important for the moment than his pursuit of Lucy. He rose at her approach, his foppish finery even more inappropriate against a background of trees than in the Pump Room.

The ladies all looked morose, as if they had not enjoyed his company. Mrs. Crane cheered up when Jessica congratulated her on the delicious repast.

"I am going for a stroll," she added, turning to Tibby.

"An excellent notion," Lord Alsop put in. "Very good for the digestion. Allow me to lend you my arm, Miss Franklin. The path is uneven."

"Thank you, sir, but Lord Ilfracombe means to escort me. We shall not go far, Aunt Tibby."

"Not out of sight, Jessica," said Miss Tibbett firmly. "If you wish to go farther, ask Nathan to go with you."

"Yes, ma'am." There was no accounting for Tibby's sense of propriety, Jessica decided, not for the first time. She would abandon her charge in a crowded ballroom without a blink, yet quibble at her taking a walk with a gentleman of unquestioned respectability and old enough to be her father. Of course, Lord Alsop was also more than old enough to be her father, and she would not trust him an inch.

Making her way back to Lord Ilfracombe, Jessica noticed that though most of the party was now standing, Matthew was still seated on the rug. His disconsolate expression drew her to his side.

"What is wrong?" she asked softly.

He grimaced. "I was caperwitted enough to sit down on the ground, and now I cannot rise without making a cake of myself."

"If I give you my hands, can you manage it?"

"Probably, but that will look as foolish as struggling up by own efforts."

She raised her voice. "I do believe that having issued a challenge, you are afraid that your cherry stones will simply drop to the ground. Come, you cannot honourably avoid the contest." She held out her hands and he took them.

With one heave he was on his feet. Jessica staggered back a step, and he caught her in his arms. For an endless moment she stared up into his face.

"Thank you," he whispered, his grey eyes warm. Then he released her and continued aloud, with a wry grin, "On the contrary, Miss Franklin, I am so certain of my superior expertise that I am reluctant to put the others to shame."

She gave him a shy smile and hurried on to join Lord Ilfracombe.

"That was well done, Miss Franklin," he said approvingly as soon as they had moved away from the others.

Jessica flushed and made a random remark about blaming Boney. She was troubled by Matthew's willingness to confess his difficulty and accept her help though he dreaded appearing crippled before the others. Right from their first meeting—their first *proper* meeting—he had been sufficiently at ease with her to talk about his wound. She had never heard him mention it in anyone else's hearing.

"I had not realized that Matthew's injury was still so troublesome," the earl was saying, confirming her thoughts. "I wonder whether his uncle knows. Surely he would not... But no matter. Boney is to blame for a great deal, is he not?"

Surely he would not have disinherited him? she wondered. With an effort she turned her attention to his comments on Napoleon's surrender to Captain Maitland of HMS *Bellerophon.*

When they returned to the picnic site, they found that the cherry stone contest had been abandoned.

"Half the stones disappeared in the grass," Nathan explained, laughing, "and as for the rest, we had endless arguments about which was whose."

"I know yours went farthest," Lucy assured him. "Jessica, you should have stayed to watch, it was such fun."

Her sparkling eyes and happy smile made Jessica look around for Lord Alsop, whose presence would have been enough to spoil her pleasure.

"He's gone," said Nathan in a low voice, reading his sister's mind. "He asked Lucy to go walking but I put a stop to that and he gave up. I never let her out of my sight, you may be sure."

And that, thought Jessica, was most satisfactory. Even Lord Alsop had his uses, if only to awake Nathan's protective instinct.

Nonetheless she was a little worried, wondering whether his lordship might be a dangerous enemy. His expression in the Pump Room, when Nathan prevented Lucy granting him a dance, had been positively malevolent, and if Nathan continued to thwart him he might seek revenge. A duel—no, she recalled his alarm at Matthew's facetious mention of pistols at dawn. He was a peer, though; perhaps he could use his influence to harm Nathan.

Lord Ilfracombe was also a peer, and a much more influential and distinguished one. He had nodded coldly to Lord Alsop on meeting him in the Pump Room, more an acknowledgement of his existence than a greeting.

"I think you are previously acquainted with Lord Alsop, sir?" Jessica asked hesitantly as she walked back into town at the earl's side.

"Very slightly." His lordship did not seem inclined to expand on the subject.

"In London?"

"Yes. He has not dared show his face there for some years, however. I was sorry to meet him in Bath and you will do well to avoid him."

"What did he do?"

"Nothing I care to discuss with a well-bred young lady, Miss Franklin," said the earl repressively. "I have reserved a box at the theatre on Tuesday next, for *A Midsummer Night's Dream.* May I hope you and your aunt will honour me with your presence?"

Jessica gracefully accepted, subject to Miss Tibbett's approval, and they went on to talk of plays and players, but not for a moment did she forget Lord Alsop. She decided to ask Matthew to find out for her what Lord Ilfracombe refused to disclose. *He* would not try to protect her from the truth only because she was a female.

She glanced back to see where he was, hoping to find an opportunity to make her request. He was flirting with Maria. Suddenly Jessica developed an absorbing interest in the relative merits of tragedy and comedy.

Not until later, at the dinner table, did Lord Ilfracombe's lack of logic strike her. "It's perfectly ridiculous," she said to Nathan and Tibby. "He would not tell me why Alsop is banned from London Society, which might be of some use to me. Yet when we spoke of Shakespeare he upheld the superior merit of tragedy, which always seems to be full of murder, mayhem and cuckoldry."

"Jessica, never say you used that word to his lordship!" Miss Tibbett was shocked.

"Mayhem?"

"No, you know very well which word I mean."

"Of course I did not, Tibby dear, nor did he speak it aloud. We talked with the utmost propriety of betrayed husbands and unfaithful wives."

Nathan laughed. "It is ridiculous, is it not? All the same, Jess, if you're determined to know all the scandal about Alsop, instead of approaching Matthew yourself I wish you will let me ask Ilfracombe. It sounds as if the baron is a decidedly loose fish."

Jessica was glad of a quiet evening at home. She settled with a book from the circulating library, but at the end of half an hour she had not the least notion what it was about. Nor had she sorted out her feelings about Matthew Walsingham, though they had occupied her mind exclusively during that period.

How close she had felt to him when he accepted her help in rising from the ground, and how distant when she heard him talking and laughing with Maria or Annabel. She must have imagined that he was especially attracted to her. Or had her recent coolness persuaded him to turn to less fickle damsels?

If so, it was just as well, she tried to convince herself. She did not want to hurt him, but she needed an unquestionably wealthy husband.

Though she made a deliberate effort to consider Lord Ilfracombe in that rôle, somehow her thoughts kept slipping back to Matthew.

CHAPTER THIRTEEN

NATHAN WAS DELVING into a plateful of kedgeree when his sister joined him at the breakfast table the next morning.

"There's a parcel for you, Jess." He pointed to the small package beside her place, wrapped in brown paper and tied with string.

"Miss Pearson's footman delivered it," Hayes informed her as he poured her tea.

"What is it?" Nathan asked, mildly interested, between mouthfuls of curried fish and rice.

"How can I tell when I can't open it?" She struggled with the knot.

"I thought it must be something Lucy said she would send you, a book or some ribbons or the like."

"No, I'm not expecting anything."

The butler produced a pair of scissors from his pocket and cut the string. Jessica unwrapped the paper and stared down in surprise at a box, some two inches by six inches, covered in blue velvet. Opening it, she gasped.

"What is it, Jess?"

Wordless, she pushed the box across the table. Nathan's hand stopped half way to his mouth, but his mouth stayed open. Diamonds and rubies glittered and glowed in the morning sunshine.

Slowly he put down his fork and picked up the bracelet. "The devil!" he said blankly.

Paper rustled as Jessica searched through the wrappings. She found a card. "Mr. Pearson, of course. It just says 'with gratitude.' Oh dear."

"Oh dear? Is that all you can say? This must be worth a fortune!"

"I daresay he bought it wholesale. After all, he was a jeweller."

Nathan dropped the fiery gems and turned his incredulous gaze on his sister. "He was *what?*"

"A jeweller. Well, actually an importer of jewels and precious metals." Jessica failed to meet his eyes but added with asperity, "Don't tell me you didn't know. He makes no attempt to keep it secret."

"I heard rumours, but I didn't think ... I didn't believe ... Dash it, Jess, if one believed all the tittle-tattle ... It's true? Lucy's father is a Cit?"

"Did you never wonder why he never accompanies her?"

"I supposed him eccentric, a recluse." Unable to sit still, he pushed his chair back and went to the window to stare blindly out at the river. "Of course I knew Lucy—Miss Pearson—is deuced fond of him, but we didn't talk about him. How long have you known?"

"A long time."

"Why did you not tell me?" he cried in anguish.

"I hoped that by the time you found out you would love Lucy enough not to mind."

"A tradesman's daughter! The Franklins have been gentry for centuries."

"It's not as if you were a peer—not even landed gentry, strictly speaking."

"Would you marry a merchant?"

"If I married a merchant I should become no more than a merchant's wife. If you marry Lucy, she will be Lady Franklin."

He was not ready for calm consideration. "Another title sold to the highest bidder. I know that was always your plan, but I had a thousand times rather lose Langdale than enter into so dishonourable an affair."

"If it were only a matter of money! But you cannot deny that you are fond of her."

"You don't understand. Or else the fellow seems to have succeeded in bribing you with diamonds to try to persuade me."

He wished the harsh words unspoken as she responded in a hurt voice, "I have every intention of returning them. I cannot possibly accept so valuable a present from an acquaintance. Nathan, surely you will not abandon Lucy to Lord Alsop?"

He swung round wildly. "Leave me alone. For pity's sake, leave me alone!" His emotions in a tumult, he rushed from the room.

Jessica heard the front door slam. She reached for the bracelet and turned it this way and that, catching the light. "Oh dear," she said again, sighing, as Miss Tibbett entered the dining room.

"Where is Sir Nathan off to in such a hurry?" Tibby enquired, taking her seat.

Jessica shook her head.

"There's been summat of an upset, madam," Hayes explained in a discreetly lowered voice, pouring tea.

Miss Tibbett nodded, glanced at the gleaming bracelet, and proceeded to spread marmalade on her toast with her usual calm. "Mr. Pearson, I assume?"

"Yes. I fear I was startled into revealing that Mr. Pearson is, or was, in trade. If I had guessed that Nathan had still not the least notion," said Jessica wretchedly, "I should have prepared him for the shock."

"That certainly explains Nathan's abrupt disappearance, but not the—ah—ornament you are holding."

"A present from Mr. Pearson, to express his gratitude, I collect. For precisely what I'm not sure. I must send it back, of course, and the sooner the better." Replacing the bracelet carefully in the box, she closed it and hooked the clasp. "Hayes, I need some new string, and please ask Tad to put his livery on to run an errand."

"I am inclined to think, Jessica, that you ought to return it in person. It appears to be an extremely valuable gift, and you will not wish Mr. Pearson to suppose that you are rejecting his gratitude, however inappropriate his mode of expressing it."

"No, but I had much rather not see Lucy. How can I possibly explain Nathan's reaction?"

"I see no need for you to disclose Nathan's reaction, so there can be no question of your attempting to explain it. If the boy has not come to his senses by the next time he sees Miss Pearson," said Tibby in her most severe governess voice, "then it will be for him to make any necessary explanations."

Jessica smiled wryly. "I keep forgetting that he's not a boy any more. Very well, I shall take this back myself."

"Shall I order a chair, Miss Jessica?" the butler enquired.

"No, I shall walk. It will give me time to work out just what I have to say to Mr. Pearson. You'll go with me, Aunt Tibby?"

Miss Tibbett looked conscious. "As a matter of fact, I had arranged to meet my friends at eleven. I could send a message..."

"No, don't do that. You cannot hold my hand while I talk to Mr. Pearson, after all. Hayes, pray tell Sukey to be ready to go with me in half an hour."

As Jessica and Sukey passed Lord Stone's house, Matthew came out of the front door, hat in hand. Seeing his smile of greeting, Jessica was aware of a sense of comfort. She banished it instantly. Since Nathan refused to marry Lucy it was up to her to save Langdale, and Matthew Walsingham could not help her.

Nonetheless, she found herself accepting his escort.

"I saw Nathan dashing off down the street earlier with a face like a thundercloud," he said, walking at her side along North Parade. "I hope there is nothing serious amiss?"

"Nothing serious." She was not quite successful at keeping the trouble from her voice.

"If there is anything I can do to help, Miss Franklin, you have only to ask." He looked down at her gravely. "In some ways, I believe, a few years service in the army postpones the attainment of maturity. Your brother is suddenly having to grow up and accept a quite different kind of responsibility from that of leading men in battle. It is not an easy process, to that I can attest. He has a good head on his shoulders, though; you need not worry that he will not find his way."

"That is very reassuring."

"Would you like me to speak to him?"

"No! Thank you, no, I think not." She could imagine few possibilities more disastrous than Nathan discussing with Matthew his refusal to marry an heiress.

"It is a sensitive matter and I fear he might blame you for interfering."

"Then let us put his problems behind us for the present. I have been reading some of the novels you recommended, and I wish you to tell me if Fanny Price is not a sad little mouse. The lively heroine of *Pride and Prejudice* is more to your taste, is she not?"

Miss Austen's works were thoroughly dissected as they walked up through the town. The weight of the bracelet in Jessica's reticule reminded her that she ought to be deciding how to return it to Mr. Pearson without offending him, but Matthew was at his most entertaining. When they reached the top of Gay Street she still had not prepared a speech.

"Would you like me to wait?" Matthew asked, as they turned into the Circus. "If you and Miss Pearson are going shopping I shall be happy to relieve Sukey of your parcels."

Though tempted, Jessica regretfully declined. "I'm not sure how long I shall be."

He knocked on the door for her, waited until the haughty butler admitted her and her maid, then went off whistling.

"Miss Pearson is still above stairs," the butler told her, "but she left orders as she's always at home to Miss Franklin. I will send to inform her of your arrival."

"It is Mr. Pearson I wish to see—privately." She was gratified to note that she had succeeded in surprising the impassive servant. One of his eyebrows twitched.

Followed by Sukey, a determined chaperone, Jessica was ushered into the sitting room to be greeted by a beaming Mr. Pearson.

"Miss Franklin, what a pleasure. . . ." His voice died away as she held out the package to him. For a moment he looked even more surprised than his butler.

"Sir, I cannot accept this. You are too generous. . . ."

"Bah, a mere bauble! You needn't think I mean anything improper by it, I just want to thank you for your kindness to Lucy. Yesterday, when she came home from the picnic, she was telling me all about such fun as she'd had. I haven't heard her laugh so carefree since I don't know when."

Jessica set the parcel on the table in the window. "I don't wish to offend you, Mr. Pearson, but indeed I cannot keep the bracelet. It simply is not *comme il faut* to accept valuable presents."

"Ah, well, if you're going to start spouting French at me, ma'am, I know when I'm beat." He sighed, yet he seemed oddly pleased. "And I'm right sorry for it. But won't you sit down, Miss Franklin, and take a dish of tea? I daresay you walked all the way up that long hill. Lucy'll be down in a trice, I make no doubt."

Glad that he was not affronted, Jessica agreed that tea would be welcome and took a seat at the table. He rang the bell, ordered tea, and joined her.

"Afore my girl comes in," he said, with a suddenly decisive air, "I want to assure you, ma'am, that if your brother was to ask me for her hand in marriage I'd not stand in his way."

It was Jessica's turn to be surprised, or rather, astonished. "I . . . but you have never met Nathan. . . ."

"I've met you, and I've heard a deal about Sir Nathan from Lucy—and others," he added obscurely. "I don't mean to press him, mind, nor her neither, and it may be I'm reading too much into what she says. She's naught but a child when all's said and done, but I'm not getting any younger myself. I married late in life, and I don't hold with it."

"I daresay you are right, sir, but you must see that I cannot speak for my brother."

"Nay, the lad has his pride, of course, and I don't think any the worse of him for that. I'd not have said a word to you, Miss Franklin, if it weren't that I'm not happy about that Lord Alsop as is making up to Lucy, not at all happy. I've found out a bit about his fine lordship since you mentioned his name to me, and it's not to his credit."

"What have you discovered?"

"The man's already been married twice, and it seems his second wife was forced to wed after he compromised her. He's a gamester with expensive tastes—ran through both wives' fortunes, mortgaged his estate to the hilt and let it go to rack and ruin. Well, the nobs'll put up with a lot if a man's born a gentleman, but Alsop ain't above marking the cards, which is what got him thrown out of his clubs. And after he refused a challenge from his second wife's brother, why, he daren't show his face in Town. Not that I approve of duelling, mind, but he's altogether a nasty piece of work."

"Good gracious, he is, is he not? If his estate is in ruins, I suppose he lives now by gambling?"

"By fleecing pigeons."

As a sheep farmer Jessica enjoyed the image conjured up by his mixed metaphor, but she was not certain what he meant. "Fleecing pigeons?"

"Swindling young men with more money than sense."

"Nathan called him a Captain Sharp."

"I heard Sir Nathan saw through him pretty quick, and it didn't do him any harm in my opinion, I can tell you."

The last thing Jessica wanted was to return to discussing her brother, so she was glad when Lucy and Mrs. Woodcock came in, followed by the butler with the tea tray.

Jessica did not see Nathan again until just before dinner. He was crossing the hall as she descended the stairs after changing her gown.

"I must talk with you," she said.

"Oh, very well, but only for a moment. I'm dining with friends and I'm already late."

She led the way into the drawing room. "I took the bracelet back to Mr. Pearson."

"Was he vexed?" Nathan sounded uninterested.

"Disappointed, in a way."

"In a way?"

"Well, I thought he seemed almost pleased, but that doesn't make sense. At least he did not press me to keep it. He told me all about Lord Alsop. He's a thorough-going scoundrel."

"Yes, I asked Lord Ilfracombe about him today." His voice held a hint of concern, Jessica thought, but it had vanished when he added impatiently, "Is that all you wanted to say?"

"Mr. Pearson is worried about Lord Alsop paying his addresses to Lucy, but he has no objection if you want to marry her."

"Has he not! I'll thank you both to keep your noses out of my affairs, you and that damned vulgar toad-eater!" Nathan flung from the room and a moment later the front door slammed behind him for the second time that day.

Jessica sank into the nearest chair.

"Has your brother gone off in a miff again?" Miss Tibbett enquired, coming in. "One might argue that such sensitivity means he is in love."

"If so, he has a poor way of showing it." Jessica told her everything. "I don't know what to do," she ended, shrugging helplessly.

"You cannot force him to offer for Miss Pearson," Tibby pointed out, "so there is no sense in worrying about it."

"None at all, only I cannot help thinking about poor Lucy—and Langdale."

Nathan did not return to escort them to the concert at the Octagon Chapel after dinner. Jessica was of two minds whether to go, but the prospect of spending the evening brooding at home was even less enticing. Her brother was not the only gentleman missing from the audience; in fact, none of the gentlemen of their particular circle were present.

It was a blushing Kitty Barlow who explained the dearth, in an excited whisper as the musicians tuned their instruments.

"Lord Peter invited them all to dinner and cards. He's going up to London tomorrow to inform his family of our betrothal."

"You are betrothed? My felicitations, Kitty dear."

"It's not official yet, not until he returns. He says that when we are properly engaged he will have neither time nor desire to entertain his male friends, so he is giving them one last party."

Knowing Lord Peter's inability to put two words together, Jessica rather doubted that he had ever expressed so complex a sentiment. Silent devotion was more his mark. He and the loquacious Kitty would probably do very well together.

"Bob is *aux anges*," Miss Barlow went on, "for once I am married he can wed his Mary. Her parents will not allow it until all his sisters are settled, you know."

Jessica had not known, and she was astonished. The music started so she was unable to explore the subject, but she was ashamed to think how she, and others, had misjudged Mr. Barlow. Friendly and obliging, he had been presumed a fortune hunter when all the time he had a sweetheart waiting at home.

Whereas no one seemed to doubt her own respectability, or Nathan's or Matthew Walsingham's, whose fortunes were all imaginary.

The strains of a Mozart piano trio banished Jessica's woes for a while, but they returned with the interval. Lucy came up to her, looking anxious.

"I noticed that Sir Nathan is not with you. Is he unwell?"

"He is spending the evening with friends. A party for gentlemen only, I collect."

Lucy blushed. "Oh, how silly of me. Of course, Mr. Barlow and Lord Ilfracombe are not here, either. But perhaps they will come soon? I saw Mr. Walsingham come in just now."

Jessica looked round and there he was, obviously making towards her in as straight a line as the chattering crowd permitted. For a moment she was overwhelmed by a yearning to tell him everything and ask his advice.

There were too many people around them. The second half of the concert began. By the time he walked home beside her sedan chair, the urge to confide had fled.

When he found out she had no fortune, would he seek elsewhere for a rich bride? Perhaps he would turn to Lucy, and Nathan would be jealous and realize how much he loved her.

She woke the next morning to a sense of *déjà vu*. Sukey was standing there with her hands on her hips, just as she had when she reported that Matthew had been disinherited. The maid's first words reinforced the impression.

"Tad says..."

"Don't tell me Tad has been gossiping at the Pig and Whistle again," said Jessica crossly.

"No, miss. It's the master, he's gone off to London. Left at first light, he did. He gave Tad this note for you."

"To London!" She sat up, unwillingly took the paper and unfolded it. "Jess," it read, "I'm off to Town with Glossop. My regiment is back in England and I want to see my friends. Don't know when I'll be back. N."

CHAPTER FOURTEEN

MATTHEW DID NOT ENJOY the performance of *A Mid-summer Night's Dream*. It was not the players' fault. Had he been sitting beside Jessica he would have thought it an excellent production. Instead, she was in the front row of the box, on the far side of Lord Ilfracombe, while he sat behind Miss Tibbett and next to a Mr. and Mrs. Fitzroy, friends of his lordship who happened to be passing through Bath.

He could see Jessica's profile as she laughed at the antics of Bottom and his fellows. Turning her head to make some comment to the earl, she flashed a smile at Matthew, but before he could respond her attention returned to the play.

With the bright stage lights behind her, her hair had a silvery shimmer. Lost in his own midsummer night's dream, he could not take his eyes off her, the curl lying intimately against her neck, her white shoulders, the graceful curve of one slender arm. Could her skin possibly be as softly satin-smooth as it looked? Perhaps it was just as well he was not sitting directly behind her.

The thunder of applause at the end of the last act took him by surprise.

"Do you wish to stay for the farce, Miss Franklin?" Lord Ilfracombe asked as the clapping died away. "I know your liking for comedy."

"If we had been watching *Othello* or *King Lear,* I should now be full of solemn, dreadful ideas instead of merriment," she pointed out. "However, 'Pyramus and Thisbe' was farce enough for me. I thought I'd die laughing when Bottom kept addressing the wall: 'O wall, O sweet and lovely wall.' I shall be quite happy to go away now—if no one else wishes to stay?"

The Fitzroys and Miss Tibbett disclaimed any desire to see the farce, so they all made their way out of the Theatre Royal. Lord Ilfracombe's carriage awaited them. His coachman stopped first at the York House Hotel, to drop off Mr. and Mrs. Fitzroy.

"I shall gladly escort Miss Tibbett and Miss Franklin home, sir," Matthew said to the earl. "There is no need for you to go any farther."

"On the contrary, it is my duty as host to see my guests safe to their front door."

The carriage set off again. The others were discussing the play, Jessica laughing again at the memory of Bottom wearing the ass's head. Matthew sat in glum silence. What was Ilfracombe's game? He monopolized Jessica's attention, deferred to her wishes, even claimed familiarity with her preferences. In fact, he was acting like a suitor. Surely the confirmed bachelor was not seriously contemplating matrimony with a girl half his age!

They reached the end of North Parade. Lord Ilfracombe handed Jessica down from the carriage, leaving Matthew to perform the same courtesy for Miss Tibbett.

"I daresay you'd have rather seen *Julius Caesar,* ma'am," he said.

"Or *Antony and Cleopatra,* or *Coriolanus,*" she agreed, a note of amusement in her voice. "All tragedies full of murder and mayhem, as Jessica would have it.''

"I am of Miss Franklin's mind. A comedy is a much pleasanter way to spend an evening.''

"Thank you, my lord, for a splendid evening,'' Jessica was saying. "I wish I could invite you and Mr. Walsingham to come in for a glass of wine, but Nathan is still away. Good night, sir.''

As the door shut behind the ladies, Lord Ilfracombe said with a frown, "I cannot like it that young Franklin is not yet returned. He ought to know better than to leave his sister unprotected.''

Matthew was going to retort that if he thought Jessica needed a man's protection he did not understand her in the least, but the earl turned away to dismiss his coachman, intending to walk back to the hotel.

"Since Miss Franklin cannot entertain us, come in with me and take a glass,'' Matthew suggested. "I'd like to talk to you.''

When they were settled before the empty grate in Lord Stone's drawing room, glasses in hand and a decanter of Lord Stone's best brandy within easy reach, he went on.

"I know it's not my place to ask this, but in Nathan's absence I'd like to know what your intentions are towards Miss Franklin.''

Lord Ilfracombe turned his snifter contemplatively, warming it between his hands. "You're right, it's not your place to ask. I shall tell you, though. I am doing my best to protect her from you.''

"From me!'' Matthew was shocked to the core. "But I love her! Do you?''

"I consider her an admirable young lady, or I should not trouble myself over her fate.''

"But you are courting her without any intention of offering for her. *I* want to marry her. You are more likely to hurt her than I."

"I am too old for her to take my attentions to heart. She has no need of my fortune, if your information is correct, and she is too sensible to be swayed by a title. Besides, I believe her to be fond of you, too fond for her own good. After all, sooner or later she must discover that you have been deceiving her."

Matthew set down his glass of brandy untouched and said gloomily, "I know it. And then she will despise me. It's a devilish coil and I don't see a way out."

"The worst of it is that I believe you and she would suit very well. Apart from this hare-brained scheme, you seem to have outgrown your taste for kicking up larks...." Ilfracombe's tone was questioning.

"I have. The most innocuous of pastimes are amusing if Jessica is there, and as for setting up a mistress, well, next to her all females are dull. But Uncle Horace would have it that I simply cannot afford riotous living any longer."

"I might have thought the same, if it wasn't for your leaving Glossop's card party to attend a concert. You were winning, too. I'll tell you what, Matthew, I'll drive out to Stone Gables some time in the next day or two and see if I cannot persuade your uncle that you are reformed."

"That's very good of you, sir. I only wish I thought you had the least chance of success."

However little hope he had, Matthew went over and over the conversation as he lay in bed that night. Though the earl's disapproval could not have changed his feelings for Jessica, he was vastly pleased that his friend approved of her, for he valued Ilfracombe's judgment.

Nonetheless, he wondered whether the earl was right in thinking that she considered him too old to be a serious suitor. His lordship was an attractive, distinguished man, and she gave every indication of enjoying his company. It was easy to say that she was too sensible to be swayed by a title, but any female would be tempted by the prospect of becoming "my lady." And though Jessica had no need for the earl's wealth, only a fool would deny that money generally weds money.

Matthew realized that he had no idea just how rich she was. Usually the size of an heiress's fortune was common knowledge to the gossipmongers: Miss Pearson, for instance, was said to have a *dot* of fifty thousand, with many times that to come on her father's demise. Though Jessica was known to be wealthy, the precise amount of her portion had escaped their calculations, perhaps because her home was in the North.

Or perhaps because her fortune was an illusion, like his own? Nathan might own a vast estate without having anything substantial to give his sister on her marriage. Lying awake tossing and turning in the small hours of the morning, Matthew found it easy to envisage the worst. Suppose she had only a thousand or two. How could he support a wife and family on the little his father had left him?

Yet he could not live without her.

Yet if she really was wealthy, she would despise him as a fortune hunter and he would lose her anyway. Uncle Horace held the only solution, and Uncle Horace never allowed himself to be persuaded. When Matthew fell asleep at last, he dreamed he was pushing Jessica in a wheelbarrow down St. James's Street. She was begging to get out, but he could not stop though Lord Stone stood directly in his path, throwing handfuls of money to the winds.

By the time he woke, Matthew's usual buoyant spirits had returned and his cheerfulness was reinforced by the letter his valet brought up with his hot water. Mr. Fitzroy wished to consult him about designing a *cottage ornée* to be built by the sea at Sidmouth, in Devon.

Forgoing breakfast, Matthew dashed over to the hotel. The Fitzroys explained their requirements and he agreed to prepare a few preliminary sketches.

Eager as he was to begin work, he stopped at the Pump Room on the way home. From the door he saw Jessica, chatting with the usual group of friends, and hurried to her side.

"You look like the cat who stole the cream," she greeted him, smiling. "Good news?"

"The Fitzroys—you recall the couple who were with us last night at the theatre?—they want me to design a house for them."

"Why, that is splendid news indeed."

"That is, they want to see my ideas for a summer villa," he corrected himself scrupulously.

"And have you any ideas?"

"Dozens, all flitting around in my head like so many butterflies."

Jessica laughed. "Then I hope you catch the best one and pin it down."

"I must go and chase them now. I wish I had time to solicit your opinion, but the Fitzroys are leaving tomorrow and want the drawings by tonight. I just wanted to tell you...."

Hazel eyes sparkling, she held out both hands to him, and as he clasped them, she said warmly, "I'm glad, and I'm delighted you have this opportunity, and I'm quite, quite certain that they will appreciate your genius and commission you to complete the design."

"And then *I* shall commission *you* to draw the façade."

"I shall be ready," she promised.

All the way back to North Parade, Matthew walked on air. In the chinks of his mind not filled with floor plans and elevations, her words echoed, "I'm glad." She shared his pleasure, she was glad he had sought her out to tell her his news, she had faith in his ability and she was ready to lend her own talent to his efforts. He could not disappoint her—the simple seaside cottage was going to be a masterpiece of its kind.

He worked hard for the rest of the day, laying out the main rooms to take advantage of the sea view while providing every possible convenience. The deep satisfaction of creating grew as the house took shape beneath his pencil. By six o'clock he was ready to present his ideas to the Fitzroys, and at seven he walked out of the York House Hotel with his first real commission in his pocket.

As he stood in the entrance, wondering whether it could by any stretch of the imagination be considered proper at this hour to go and tell Jessica of his triumph, Bob Barlow came towards him.

"Evening, Walsingham." His round face was sunk in gloom. "I've heard from Glossop."

"Bad news?"

"His mother wants to see our Kitty before the family decides whether to accept her into their august ranks."

"That's only natural." In his present exalted mood, Matthew was inclined to look for silver linings to every cloud.

"The marchioness is a real Tartar, high in the instep as they come, and Glossop's terrified of her. Bravest thing he's ever done, tackling her. She's coming down to Bath in a couple of weeks, he says. Lord knows when I'll be able to wed my Mary."

"At least the Glossops haven't rejected your sister out of hand," Matthew pointed out. Barlow was a good fellow, and anyone who struggled with such persistence against all obstacles deserved to win the lady of his choice. "Come and share a bottle to cheer you up."

They went into the tap-room and Matthew called for a bottle of claret.

"I don't mind telling you it's been a long wait," Barlow confided, swigging his wine. "Two years since Mary and I plighted our troth. Her parents won't let us get spliced until all my sisters have caught themselves husbands, and Kitty's the last of 'em. We'll miss Kitty when she's gone, but there will be room enough in my father's house to set up a second household. I daresay you'll not have that problem, eh? Plenty of space at Stone Gables, or there's always the house here in Bath." He sighed. "Ah, well, riches to riches, it's the way of the world."

"Riches to riches?" Matthew asked cautiously, refilling Barlow's glass and sipping at his own.

"You and Miss Franklin. Oh, I know there's nothing been announced, but it's plain as a pikestaff there's a match in the making. Lord Stone owns half Somerset and Sir Nathan has vast estates in the North—a deuced eligible connexion. And then there's what she'll get from the old aunt, you lucky devil."

"From Miss Tibbett? What makes you suppose that so eccentric a lady has anything worth leaving?"

"Stands to reason, don't it? Only rich old biddies can afford to have a bee in the bonnet. And she practically brought the girl up so I shouldn't think there's much doubt where the rhino'll go." Mr. Barlow, having emptied his glass for the third time, became contemplative. "Wonder if old Pearson's going to pull it off. Sharp as a needle, won't give just anyone his daughter and her fortune, but looks as if he's let Franklin slip the hook."

Matthew took this somewhat muddled statement to mean that Mr. Pearson, a careful man, approved Nathan as his son-in-law, but that Nathan cavilled at marrying a Cit's daughter. "Did Glossop say when he's returning from Town?" he asked. "I imagine Franklin will come back with him."

"Daresay." Barlow nodded in amicable agreement. "Glossop's a fine catch for our Kitty, no mistake. Com...comf'able comp'tence and she'll be her la'ship. If his ma'll have her. High in the instep, y'know."

"So you said. I daresay she will be glad to see him settled with so amiable a bride as your sister," Matthew assured him, and steered him homeward.

By the time he reached North Parade, it was definitely too late to call at Number 15. Jessica and Miss Tibbett would be sitting down to their dinner, and Matthew was hungry for his. There was no assembly that night. He could have dropped in after dinner if Nathan had been at home, but as it was he'd have to wait until the morning to tell her about his commission.

He hoped Nathan would come back soon. As he sat down to a fragrantly steaming steak and kidney pie, he realized that Bob Barlow had not said when Glossop was expected.

He had said a great many other things, though. What impressed Matthew most was that Mr. Pearson favoured Nathan. The shrewd merchant was not likely to be taken in by false claims, so Matthew's doubts about Jessica's wealth had been as chimerical as most midnight worries.

Now all he had to worry about was how to confess his own deception without earning her utter contempt.

There was no sign of contempt when he called at Number 15 at the earliest decent hour next morning. Jessica was as pleased as he could have wished at his good news. Together they pored over his preliminary designs for the cottage, and she made several suggestions, a number of which he vowed to adopt, to her evident gratification.

"Wooden shutters against winter storms blowing in off the sea are a particularly good notion," he said. "They will add character to the exterior, too. But I draw the line at a widow's walk on the roof. The villa is a summer retreat for the landed gentry, not a home for a sea-captain's wife."

"It might be bought one day by a sailor, and then what is his wife to do when his ship is overdue?" she argued with spirit. "Besides, it will make a pleasant, breezy place to stroll on hot days."

"I'll suggest it to the Fitzroys," he offered.

"Fair enough."

Miss Tibbett peered at him over her spectacles. "A roofed peristyle running the length of the frontage would provide a more convenient place to exercise," she pointed out. Warming to her theme, she pushed the spectacles up onto her head and continued, "Since it would be shaded, one might also sit there to enjoy both air and view, and think what dignity a few Roman pillars would add to your façade."

"It's supposed to be a simple cottage, Aunt Tibby," Jessica protested, laughing. "You will have it looking like a temple to Neptune."

"A full peristyle might be going a little too far," Matthew agreed, "but the Neptune idea is worth exploring. How about a mosaic of a Triton blowing his horn over the front door?"

They discussed the pros and cons, with Miss Tibbett contributing learned comments on the Romans' use of mosaics. She even produced a book with copies of a number of tessellated floors found in Britain.

"I am sure there is one of Neptune," she said, reaching for her spectacles.

Jessica had to disentangle them from her hair before she could search the volume for the desired drawing. That was not the first time Matthew had seen the operation performed and he admired Jessica's patience. He admired her pragmatic interest in his work, her imaginative suggestions and her sparkling eyes when she defended them, the way she tilted her head when considering an idea, the sheen of her ash-blonde tresses, her graceful movements....

Needless to say, when invited to stay for luncheon, he accepted.

He had hoped to take Jessica for a drive in his curricle that afternoon—with Hanson in attendance, of course—but it began to rain. Not wanting to outstay his welcome, he went home and did some work on the Sidmouth villa plans. He was still at the dining table some hours later, wrestling with a recalcitrant staircase, when the door knocker sounded.

"Lord Ilfracombe," his valet announced.

Matthew rose eagerly. He had not seen his friend since the Fitzroys gave him the commission. However, the earl got his news in first.

"I've been to Stone Gables."

"Have you, sir! Take a seat and tell me all, or shall we remove to the drawing room?"

"This will do very well." Ilfracombe sat down at the table and pulled one of Matthew's drawings towards him. "You too have been busy, I see."

"Yes, the Fitzroys." He nodded to his servant, who was hovering with an enquiring look near the door. "The madeira, Renfrew. It was devilish good of you, sir, to show them the work I did for you. I am to design a house for them. What happened at Stone Gables? Is Uncle Horace still incensed against me?"

"I saw Miss Stone first, and she warned me not to mention your name in your uncle's presence."

"He is unrelenting, then." Though Matthew had not expected the earl's efforts in his behalf to be effective, he could not pretend he was not disappointed. "How is Aunt Caro?"

"She has not changed in twenty years. Her beauty is from within, and time cannot alter it." The faraway look in his lordship's eyes faded as Renfrew entered with glasses and a decanter of Uncle Horace's madeira. Accepting a glass of wine, he went on, "And after twenty years you still retain her affection. She is fighting for you."

"Fighting?"

"Perhaps plotting is the word I want. At any rate, she invited your cousin Biggin to visit, and having made him his heir, Lord Stone was not in a position to object."

Matthew frowned. "I heard Cousin Archibald was there. One of my uncle's grooms was here overnight and he mentioned it to Hanson—my groom. Archie's not popular with the servants, I collect, but I cannot see how that helps me."

"How well do you know him? How often do you see him?"

"As rarely as possible," said Matthew promptly. "His—er—brand of piety is not to my taste."

"It's not to the viscount's taste, either. His preaching against strong drink is driving your uncle to the bottle, and his preaching in favour of Christian charity is enough to try even your aunt's sweet temper."

"Poor Aunt Caro!"

"Miss Stone feels that though it is impossible to prove to her brother that you are a paragon of virtue, it is quite possible to prove that a paragon of virtue is not what he really wants as his heir."

"He may dislike Archie's preaching, but he has always been a strong upholder of the Church of England. He has three livings in his gift, and he's always been at great pains to find devout and deserving incumbents, even if he sleeps through their sermons once they are appointed. To turn against Cousin Archibald because of his piety would make him look foolish, if not hypocritical, and Uncle Horace cannot abide being made to look a fool."

"He'll look a worse fool if he's forced to ban his heir from his house to get a bit of peace. I tell you, after half an hour in your cousin's company I was ready to slaughter the fellow out of hand."

"I know what you mean," said Matthew, grinning.

"It is therefore with extreme misgiving that I shall drive over again next week to reassess the situation. I trust you are duly grateful."

"Indeed I am, and I shall stand character witness when you are tried for murder. I suppose it's possible that Uncle Horace might be driven by desperation to disinherit him. The trouble is, that doesn't mean I should be reinstated. Archie and I are his closest relatives, being his sisters' sons, but there are dozens of cousins of varying degree. Since there's no question of an entail, he'd probably pick one of them, or divide his worldly wealth among the lot."

CHAPTER FIFTEEN

"NOTHING EVER SEEMS to change," said Jessica gloomily, abandoning a letter to one of her real aunts and staring out of the window at the rain dimpling a puddle in the street.

"It has been raining for days," Miss Tibbett concurred.

"It's not just the rain. Nathan came back from London a fortnight since but he's no nearer to offering for Lucy. He treats her just as he did before he left."

"Miss Pearson appears to find his conduct acceptable."

"His presence is better than his absence, I suppose, though I don't doubt the poor girl would find a little more ardour to her liking."

"Not without a declaration to follow." Miss Tibbett set down her book and eyed her "niece" severely over her spectacles.

"Naturally. And Mr. Walsingham pursues me as ardently as ever, yet he, too, seems no nearer to a declaration. Nor, in the circumstances, am I sure what I should say if he did offer." She sighed.

"And Lord Ilfracombe? An eminently eligible gentleman."

"I doubt he'll come up to scratch. If he did—I don't know. I like him, and marrying him would solve all our problems, but even were he not so much older than I, I fear his attempts to shelter me would stifle me. He was truly shocked that we had no gentleman to protect us while Nathan was in London."

"A very proper sentiment, though scarcely calculated to find favour in your eyes. I sometimes wonder if your father was correct in refusing to let me curb your independent spirit."

"Oh, Tibby, as if you could have when you are just as independent-minded." With quick, light steps Jessica crossed the room and hugged her mentor, then sat down beside her on the green brocade sofa. "I don't know what I should have done without you. But if we lose Langdale, we shan't be able to pay your salary any longer."

"My dear, you must not worry about me. My friends are going to spend the winter in Italy, now that Bonaparte is gone and travel is possible again, and they have invited me to go with them."

"Your clergyman and his wife? That's wonderful! You will see Rome at last."

"I must confess that I am anticipating the visit with extraordinary enthusiasm." Miss Tibbett's eyes gleamed above her spectacles. "When I return I shall seek another post or, if it proves possible, I shall come to you. Owing to your father's generosity, I have saved nearly every penny of my salary these fifteen years and I shall be able to contribute to your household rather than being a drain on its resources."

Tears in her eyes, Jessica hugged her again, to the imminent peril of the spectacles. "I'm so glad. I could not bear to lose you. But there's no knowing what sort of household it will be, or if there will be a household at all, unless something changes in the next two or three weeks. We cannot stay in Bath much longer."

"Did you not reckon that the proceeds from the sale of your diamonds were sufficient to last until Michaelmas?"

"We have enough money, barely, but when I proposed to stay here until the end of September I had not considered all there is to be done if we have to leave Langdale. The sheep will have to be sold, as well as all the furniture we shan't need in our new home—and we must find a new home. The servants must be given notice, and pensions arranged for those too old to seek posts elsewhere."

"Of course. A month will scarcely be time enough to settle everything."

"I expect we ought also to give Mr. Scunthwaite a month's notice so that he can find another tenant."

"I do not consider that you owe that man any particular courtesy," said Miss Tibbett with unwonted indignation, "since he is doing his best to drive you from your home and reduce you to living in a cottage!"

"Living in a cottage will not be so bad, will it? I hope to be able to keep Sukey and Tad with us. Only I cannot imagine Nathan being content with nothing to do. I daresay he will rejoin the army, in which case I suppose I shall have no choice but to go to live with relatives. What a horrid fate! Perhaps I shall accept Lord Ilfracombe after all, if he offers in time."

However, far from being on the brink of a proposal, Lord Ilfracombe seemed less and less determined in his pursuit of Jessica. In fact he was positively elusive, absenting himself from Bath several times a week. He mentioned once or twice that he had driven out to Stone Gables to visit Lord Stone. Matthew had not gone with him, confirming, in Jessica's opinion, the breach between uncle and nephew.

Precious time was passing, and nothing changed except the weather.

It stopped raining at last. Instead of scurrying under umbrellas, Jessica and Nathan enjoyed the stroll to the Pump Room to see their friends.

On the second fine morning, Kitty Barlow told Jessica that they were expecting the arrival that evening of the Marchioness of Leighton. She seemed undismayed at the prospect of facing her beloved's haughty mama, but Lord Peter was decidedly apprehensive. Standing nearby, Matthew and Nathan were doing their best to distract him.

Then Matthew turned to the ladies and announced, "Glossop agrees with me that we must take advantage of the fair weather while we may and go boating on the canal this afternoon."

Lord Peter looked surprised but obligingly muttered, "Cambridge...punt..." and cast a pleading glance at Kitty.

"An excellent notion," she assured him, and he relaxed. Nathan seconded her, and set about persuading Lucy to go, a task he accomplished without much difficulty. They went off to obtain Mrs. Woodcock's permission. Kitty took Lord Peter in search of her mother, leaving Jessica with Matthew.

She was feeling annoyed that her participation seemed to be taken for granted, when he said anxiously, "I hope this afternoon is convenient for you, Miss Franklin? Otherwise I shall have to run after them and change the date. You did promise to go with me one day."

"I am not otherwise engaged," she admitted. "But I shall have to see if Aunt Tibby is willing to chaperone us. I cannot imagine Mrs. Woodcock or Mrs. Barlow in a punt, can you?''

"Lord, no!" He grinned at her, the boyish grin that had first attracted her when he was a stranger driving by. "Miss Tibbett is equal to anything, though."

And so it proved. At the Sydney Wharf a few hours later Miss Tibbett, discoursing knowledgeably on Roman shipping, allowed Mr. Barlow to assist her into a hired skiff. Jessica joined her, and Bob Barlow and Matthew took up the oars while the other four members of the party embarked in a punt.

While Nathan was occupied in making sure Kitty and Lucy were comfortable, Lord Peter pushed off with the punt pole. The rain-washed air sparkled in the sunshine and the still, greenish waters of the canal swirled and gurgled as the boats began to move between the steep banks. For a few moments Jessica watched Matthew with unacknowledged anxiety, but rowing did not seem to cause him any discomfort.

She caught his eye.

"Waiting for me to catch a crab, Miss Franklin?" he teased. "I rowed at Eton, you know."

"Catch a crab?" she asked uncertainly. "I doubt there are any in the canal."

Matthew laughed.

"It means to dig too deep with an oar," Bob Barlow explained, "thus spoiling the stroke and usually soaking everyone in the boat."

Jessica looked down at her new India muslin. "Perhaps I should have embarked in the punt," she said, glancing across at the other vessel.

Lord Peter, near as long and thin as his pole, was propelling the punt along with stylish ease, while Nathan watched enviously.

"I see how to do it. Let me take a turn."

"Tunnel," said Lord Peter. "After that."

The black mouth of the tunnel loomed ahead. Lucy looked at it nervously, giving Nathan an excuse to take her hand for reassurance, though the far end was already visible as they floated under the arch.

"Hoo!" called Bob Barlow.

"Hoo, hoo, hoo," returned the echo, and within moments they were all shouting so loud the echo had no chance to reply.

"Disgraceful, children," said Miss Tibbett with a smile as the boats emerged into sunshine dappled with wavering tree-shadows.

The trees grew high above them atop the stone walls of the Sydney Gardens cutting, sheer on one side with just enough level ground on the other for the towpath. On the two ornamental bridges ladies and gentlemen leaned against the iron railings, looking down at the boaters. Kitty recognized an acquaintance and waved vigorously.

Three small children waved back. "Look, Peter," cried Kitty. "The little darlings!"

At the same time Nathan was saying, "I'll take my turn now...."

Distracted, Lord Peter lost his rhythm. Jessica never worked out just how it happened, but suddenly there he was dangling from the punt pole while the boat floated serenely onward. The pole wavered back and forth. Lord Peter's pantaloon-clad legs scrabbled frantically for a foothold on thin air, and then he hit the water with a splash and disappeared beneath the murky surface.

"...Or perhaps I won't," Nathan continued, tearing off his coat and hat and diving to the rescue.

Scarcely taking time to ship his oars, Matthew also flung himself into the canal. He and Nathan converged on the spot where Lord Peter had gone down, arriving just as his lordship's long face reappeared, spluttering.

"All right," he gasped. "Not deep."

Indeed he seemed to have found firm footing, his narrow shoulders breaking the water. A moment later Matthew also put his feet down. The water came to his chin. Following their example, Nathan vanished from the nose down.

Matthew and Lord Peter each seized him by an invisible arm and hoisted him above the surface.

"It's all right, I'll swim," he told them. They both let go. Nathan disappeared again, then bobbed up, treading water. "Are you trying to drown me?" he asked indignantly.

All three seemed safe now. Jessica let out her breath on a snort of laughter and Bob Barlow guffawed.

"I regret spoiling the show," Miss Tibbett intervened, "but Miss Barlow and Miss Pearson are in something of a pickle."

Lord Peter's final push had impelled the punt a surprising distance. In it sat Lucy and Kitty, stranded without means of propulsion.

"Help!" wailed Lucy.

"Do something, Bob," Kitty ordered.

Matthew and Nathan started swimming after them, while Lord Peter appeared to be walking along the bottom, breasting the ripples like a large and ungainly duck. Bob Barlow bent to his oars.

"Watch out!" Jessica cried, heart in mouth as one heavy wooden blade passed within inches of Matthew's right ear. Mr. Barlow promptly caught a crab, showering her and Miss Tibbett with sparkling droplets. "My new muslin," she mourned.

Nathan reached the punt and grasped the side. It tilted alarmingly. Lucy and Kitty squealed, hanging on to the other side for dear life. Matthew stood up and steadied the boat while Nathan clambered aboard. Lucy and Kitty squealed again, cowering back in an attempt to protect their muslins.

"Well, I like that!" said Nathan, sitting up amidships. "No thanks for the rescue?"

Lucy gave him a handkerchief and he wiped his face with the tiny, lacy scrap of linen.

"How are you proposing to rescue us when you have neither oars nor pole?" Kitty enquired with interest.

"Lord Peter shall tow you," Matthew proposed, grinning. Lord Peter was making heavy weather of it, pushing through the water slowly but perseveringly.

Jessica was helpless with laughter, quite unable to give Bob Barlow directions as he rowed on, his back to his destination. Fortunately Miss Tibbett was in control of herself and the situation. She steered around Lord Peter and commanded sharply, "Ship oars!" at precisely the right moment. The skiff floated onward to nudge gently against the punt's stern.

A burst of clapping from above reminded everyone they had an audience. Lord Peter—at last arriving on the scene—and Lucy both blushed fiery red, while Jessica exchanged a rueful glance with Matthew. This expedition could not possibly be less than a nine days' wonder, and it might very likely go down in the annals of Bath.

"My hat!" yelped Lord Peter, clapping a hand to his bare head. He gazed mournfully back at the spot where his once-glossy beaver bobbed like a fisherman's buoy.

Crouching in the middle of the punt, Nathan was shivering. Though Jessica doubted her brother would come to harm on such a warm day, she was concerned for Matthew. She had long since ceased to notice his limp—and to believe in his weak chest—but a dousing in the remarkably cold waters of the canal was not going to do him any good. His face was pale and drawn. The sooner he was out of there the better.

Heedless now of her new gown, Jessica scrambled to the skiff's bow and picked up the boathook. "Nathan, help me turn the boats around. We'll have to tow you back."

"How am I supposed to help? Give me a pair of oars and I'll row."

"You haven't got those things to rest the oars in."

"Rowlocks," supplied Matthew. "Dashed difficult to row without 'em." He tugged on the side of the punt and it began to turn. Lord Peter went to his assistance.

Bob Barlow decided not to wait for help. He lowered his oars into the water again and began a complicated manoeuvre involving paddling backwards with one and forwards with the other. Slowly the skiff swung about.

"Watch out!" shrieked Jessica, heart in mouth as one heavy wooden blade passed within inches of Matthew's left ear.

Both boats were broadside on across the canal when a large brown horse plodded round a bend in the towpath, followed by a gaily painted barge. The horse, an intelligent creature, stopped dead in its tracks on seeing the obstruction. The barge, obedient to Isaac Newton's laws, slid onward.

Losing his head, Bob Barlow confused his backward oar with his forward oar. The skiff shot forward and Jessica only just managed to fend it off from the punt with her boathook. Horrified, she looked round to see if it had decapitated Lord Peter, as had seemed inevitable.

Lord Peter had ducked. He rose from the waves, spluttering.

"Here, I say!" he protested.

Jessica fended off from the bank, in the process completing the skiff's turn. They were now in a good position to take the punt in tow—if it wasn't for the barge rapidly bearing down on them.

The bargee, in his breeches, short coat, and flat-crowned hat, was joined on deck by his wife and two children. They watched expressionlessly as their craft advanced on the hapless boaters. In the narrow cutting there was no room for the long, unwieldy vessel to manoeuvre.

The barge glided to a halt close enough for Jessica to count every red petal and green leaf painted on her blue and yellow deck house, to read her gold-scrolled name, the *Marybelle*, out of Reading. It was the wrong moment to ponder the engineering marvel that had connected the Avon with the Kennet (and thus the Thames), Bristol with London across the width of England.

"Well now," said the bargee unhelpfully.

The horse ambled into view and cast on the scene a glance of ineffable scorn before turning its head to nibble at a tuft of grass growing between the stones of the wall.

Nathan tossed the punt's painter to Matthew.

He made it fast to the skiff's stern, then said with studied nonchalance, "I believe I shall walk, if you can manage on your own, Barlow? I dread to think what may happen if I try to climb into the boat."

"No, no, don't," exclaimed Mr. Barlow with a shudder. "I'll do it all right."

Matthew and Lord Peter made their way to the bank, pushed and hauled each other out of the canal, and set off along the towpath, dripping. The horse snorted derisively as they passed.

With Jessica and Nathan wielding the boathooks, Bob Barlow, his round face red from exertion, succeeded in rowing the two boats past the barge. A rousing cheer wafted down from the bridges.

Jessica waved to the spectators. "Show them you think it all a good joke," she called softly to the three in the punt. "Wave."

Nathan obeyed with a grin, and after a moment Kitty did likewise. Lucy raised a timid hand in a sort of half-salute. Jessica was satisfied. If the participants in the disaster laughed at their own misadventures, the roasting they were bound to receive would be friendly instead of humiliating. And there was no denying, she thought with a giggle, that some of it had been very funny indeed.

She was not at all inclined to be amused when they passed the stern of the barge and she saw Matthew on the towpath. Limping badly, he looked exhausted. While she hesitated, not wanting to draw attention to his disability in front of the others, Miss Tibbett took a hand.

"I see no reason why Lord Peter and Mr. Walsingham should be unable to embark safely from the bank," she remarked. "Can you draw alongside, Mr. Barlow?"

"If I can't we're going to be in trouble when we reach the wharf," he grunted.

Their luck had turned. They pulled up smoothly to the bank and the two sodden gentlemen lowered themselves with utmost care into the boats, which did no worse than rock gently.

Jessica pushed off, then handed Matthew his beaver and her handkerchief, embroidered with pink rosebuds. Even wet, his dark hair curled, she noticed.

He gave her a wry grin as he dried his hair as best he could and put on his hat. "The next time I take you boating, Miss Franklin," he said, "it will be in a steam packet on the Thames and we shall sit in the centre of the deck, as far from the water as possible."

At that precise moment she knew without a shadow of doubt that, given half a chance, she would marry him if he were a penniless beggar.

She had no time to think about the implications. As they entered the dark of the tunnel, Bob Barlow's steering became erratic again and she was busy with the boathook. Then they emerged into brilliant sunshine and Sydney Wharf lay ahead. The men working there turned and stared as the bedraggled boatloads approached.

"Us'll have to charge you extry fer takin' a dip," said one wit. "A-drinkin' of the waters, too, was you?"

They all guffawed, but they helped pull the boats into the dock and handed the ladies out with rough and ready courtesy.

Matthew's curricle, Lord Peter's phaeton and Mr. Pearson's splendid barouche awaited them. In no condition to follow the promptings of gallantry, the three wet, shivering gentlemen at once drove off to find hot baths and dry clothes. Bob Barlow handed the ladies into the barouche and took his seat beside his sister. The coachman turned towards Pulteney Bridge.

"Do you think Sir Nathan will be all right?" asked Lucy anxiously. Sitting between Jessica and Miss Tibbett, she turned to first one then the other for reassurance. "You will tell me, will you not, if he should take a fever?"

For the rest of the way to North Parade, Jessica was occupied in trying to convince Lucy that Nathan was as strong as an ox. In this she was aided by Miss Tibbett's reminiscences about the shocking scrapes he had fallen into as a boy without taking any harm.

"I guarantee he will be there to dance with you at the assembly tonight," Jessica said at last as she stepped down from the barouche. Pausing on the pavement, she waved farewell as the carriage drove off, but her eyes were on Matthew's front door. "I suppose it would not be proper to send Tad to see how Mr. Walsingham does," she said to Tibby with a sigh.

"No, and if you did you would likely get no answer but 'Very well.' You had best persuade your brother to call on him later," suggested Miss Tibbett understandingly, leading the way into the house.

They went upstairs to change their gowns. The canal water had dried to dirty grey-green splotches, but Sukey was sure the India muslin could be saved with careful laundering. Jessica regaled the maid with the tale of the calamitous outing.

Sukey chuckled at the antics of her purported betters, then said sagely, "I 'spect the cold water weren't too good for the poor gentleman's leg. Mrs. Ancaster better send Tad over to borrow an onion or some such from his housekeeper and find out what's what."

"Bless you, Sukey," her mistress said, and kissed her.

Pink with pleasure, the girl carried off the soiled gown. Jessica curled up in her favourite seat, by the window overlooking the Avon. Musing, she watched a pair of swans proudly lead their near-fledged cygnets up the river. Serene and haughty in their pure white plumage, they seemed to glide without effort, but beneath the surface their feet must be paddling vigorously against the current.

Cob and pen mated for life, she knew. How did they choose their mates? Surely without all the toil and heartache foolish humans brought to the problem!

To an onlooker, how carefree her life must appear: strolling about the Pump Room, boating on the canal, dancing the night away. Beneath the surface she was struggling against the current. She could not admit her deception to Matthew. To do so would be tantamount to revealing that she loved him, a course no well-bred young lady could contemplate with anything but horror. Yet as long as he thought her wealthy, confession must be equally difficult for him.

Did he have the courage—did he love her enough—to tell her the truth?

CHAPTER SIXTEEN

"...AND THE HOUSEKEEPER made him a linseed poultice, Miss Jessica," Tad reported, "and he's resting."

Though she had hoped to hear that Matthew was in fine twig, Jessica was relieved that at least he had acknowledged his discomfort and allowed his housekeeper to try a remedy. She thanked Tad and turned back to the plans of the summer villa, setting useless worry aside for the moment.

Matthew had given her his plans a couple of days ago, but she had not had time to look at them. She was impressed. The design seemed to her both imaginative and practical. With Lord Ilfracombe's patronage he would have no difficulty making a living, she thought hopefully. And as she set about studying the drawings with a view to sketching the façade, she recalled that Nathan had said jokingly that she and Matthew should go into partnership. She would not be a burden—she would help him in his work.

Nathan came into the dining room, looking none the worse for his ducking. "I'm off to return Lucy's handkerchief," he announced. "Sukey washed and ironed it for me." Carefully he tucked the lace-trimmed square into his pocket.

"I'm sure she will be happy to receive it," said his sister ironically. Matthew had *her* handkerchief, and she would not be at all pleased if he insisted on giving it back. She'd much prefer him to carry it always next to his heart.

Nathan was as impervious to irony as he was to cold water. Jessica heard him whistling as he crossed the hall, then the click of the latch as the front door closed quietly behind him. She sang to herself as she began a rough sketch.

"Although if I pleased I might marry with ease,
For where maidens are fair many suitors will come,
Oh, he whom I wed must be North-country bred
And carry me back to my North-country home."

That wasn't what she wanted, though. Married to Matthew, she wouldn't care in the least where they lived. She consulted the elevation; the shutters were a nice touch. Perhaps they could find a cottage by the sea?

"The oak and the ash and the bonny ivy tree,
They flourish at home..."

The door knocker sounded, followed by a sort of fumbling rush of feet that she recognized as Tad struggling into his livery coat on his way to answer it.

He appeared at the dining room door. "It's Miss Pearson, miss."

"Show her in, please, Tad." Jessica rose as Lucy came in, carrying a withy basket. "My dear, what brings you back so soon?"

Lucy blushed. "I told Papa and Mrs. Woodcock how Sir Nathan dived into the canal to save Lord Peter, and Mrs. Woodcock gave me a receipt for a gruel to ward off a chill."

"How kind of you to bring it." Jessica omitted to point out that she could have sent a footman, and failed to inform her that not only was Nathan in the pink of health but he would not touch gruel if he were at death's door.

"After you strain out the oatmeal," Lucy explained, "you put in lemon juice and soda to make it fizz like champagne, so it has to be drunk as soon as it is made. I brought all the ingredients and I thought—in case your cook is busy—I might make it myself?"

"I'm afraid Nathan has gone..."

The door swung open and Nathan burst in. "Jess, is Lucy... Miss Pearson! I saw your carriage in York Street as I turned into the Abbey Yard, so I came back. Is anything wrong?"

"Oh no, sir, if you are well." Lucy's blush deepened. "I was afraid you might take cold so I brought a receipt for a special gruel. I wanted to make it for you myself, but I see you do not need it."

"I do feel a slight tickle in my throat," said Nathan heroically.

"Then off with you both to the kitchen," Jessica urged, hiding a smile. "Mrs. Ancaster will be glad to see you."

They were gone for nearly an hour. When they returned, Nathan reported that the gruel was not so bad after all, rather like fizzy lemonade, and that Mrs. Ancaster had fed them on blackcurrant tarts.

"And she gave me some blackcurrant cordial," said Lucy, producing from her basket a small, corked bottle. "But she said she bought the currants in the market so it will not be as good as if you had picked them fresh in the gardens at Langdale, with the dew still on them. Did you really pick your own currants, Jessica?''

"Yes, but rarely early enough to catch the dew!''

"That sounds like fun.''

"It is, if you don't mind having red-stained fingers for the rest of the day.''

"I should not mind. I think I should like to have a garden, and learn to make cordials and jellies and jams.'' She sighed softly, with a sidelong glance at Nathan, but he was frowning down at Jessica's half-completed sketch. "I must go now. It's nearly time to change for dinner and the assembly.''

Nathan escorted her to her carriage. Jessica put away the drawings and was just leaving the dining room when he came back in. In his hand was a small, white, lacy square, which he regarded not with the annoyance of someone who has forgotten something but with a complacent smile.

On seeing Jessica, he quickly thrust Lucy's handkerchief back into his pocket and said with a false air of nonchalance, "Mrs. Woodcock's gruel worked. The tickle in my throat is quite gone away.''

"You surprise me," said Jessica, laughing.

She was thoughtful, though, as she went up the stairs to her chamber to change for dinner. Nathan and Lucy were obviously made for each other. Nathan's stubborn persistence in his prejudice against her father bid fair to ruin both their lives. He was much too sure of her, too. He needed a rival to spur him to action, but even Lord Alsop no longer paid his addresses to Lucy— at least in Nathan's presence.

Jessica decided it was up to her to apply the spur, and she had an inkling of an idea how to do it.

She forgot all about Nathan and Lucy when Sukey asked which gown she wanted to wear to the assembly. Her thoughts flew to Matthew. Was he well enough to attend? If not, she didn't want to go.

"Mrs. Ancaster sent Tad over to pay back the onion she borrowed," volunteered Sukey, apparently reading her mistress's mind. "Seems Mr. Walsingham's up and about and his man's a-polishing his dancing shoes."

The nagging worry that had been hovering behind Jessica's conscious thoughts vanished like a soap bubble. "I'll wear the blue with the silver tasselled sash," she said.

Matthew arrived at Number 15 just as they finished dinner.

"I shall drive to the Assembly Rooms tonight," he explained. "May I hope to be permitted to take up Miss Franklin?"

"Oh yes, the curricle is much more comfortable than a chair," Jessica assured him.

"I was not inviting you," he retorted, his eyes laughing at her. "I was asking permission of your aunt and your brother."

She pouted at him.

"Very proper of you, Mr. Walsingham," said Miss Tibbett. "I suppose you will take your groom?"

"Naturally, ma'am. I hoped that unfortunate incident had been forgiven and forgotten."

"Of course it has, it was only the once, after all," said Nathan, and added grandly, "You have my permission."

Jessica snorted in a most unladylike manner. "The day I ask your permission, brother mine, will be the day pigs fly."

The gentlemen exchanged glances.

"There's a balloon ascension from Sydney Gardens next week," said Matthew.

"I daresay I could find a farmer willing to lend a pig," said Nathan.

"Odious wretches!" Jessica cried. "I wager you'll not so easily persuade the aeronaut to take a pig with him! Give me five minutes, sir, and I shall be ready to go."

She went to fetch her silver gauze shawl, her fan and gloves and reticule. When she descended the stairs, he was waiting in the hall, watch in hand. He looked up at her with what she trusted was bemused admiration.

"Five minutes to the second, Miss Franklin." He offered his arm as Tad opened the front door.

"I hoped you were admiring my appearance, not my punctuality," she said tartly.

"Punctuality is a virtue, beauty a mere attribute."

"I see you are in a teasing humour tonight, sir. I shall therefore regale you with a description of your appearance when you emerged from the canal this afternoon."

Driving through the town towards the Upper Rooms, they laughed over the ill-fated expedition. Jessica was reluctant to mention the effect of the cold water on his injured leg, and she was glad when he brought up the subject himself.

"I feared for a while that the ducking had done for me," he said with a rueful smile.

"So did I. It was a great relief when you turned up on our doorstep on your own two feet."

"I shall not dance tonight, however. Will you mind sitting out the two sets you promised me? It is a lot to ask, I know, and I shall release you if you insist."

"How can I decently insist when you put it like that? You ought to have released me from my promise first, so that I could be noble and offer to keep you company instead of dancing."

"But you might not have been feeling noble, and then I should have lost the pleasure of your company," he pointed out.

"Are you expressing doubts as to the nobility of my nature, Mr. Walsingham?" Jessica enquired archly, then wished she hadn't. There was nothing noble about the part she and Nathan were playing. "No, don't tell me. I might not like the answer. I shall certainly sit out two dances with you, if you will protect me from all the quizzing that is bound to come our way."

"My way. I was the one who jumped in, after all."

"On a noble mission of rescue. I wonder how poor Lord Peter will face the roasting—oh no, his mama arrives tonight, does she not? He will not come to the assembly."

Bob Barlow met them at the door, a joyful beam on his round face. "Miss Franklin, pray stand up with me for the cotillion. I am deputed by my sister to give you her news."

"You look pleased as Punch," said Matthew. "Am I not to hear it?"

"A young lady's confidences are not to be imparted to all and sundry," Jessica informed him. "I shall tell you later as much as I consider fit for a gentleman's ears."

"Lady Leighton arrived early and it's all settled," said Mr. Barlow jubilantly. "Kitty is with her now. Come, ma'am, the music is starting."

"Without prejudice to your sister," Jessica said as they made their way through the crowd onto the floor,

"I am amazed that the marchioness is so soon satisfied of her merits."

"It all fell out most handily. Poor Glossop arrived at his lodging dripping wet to find her ladyship awaiting him."

"How very disconcerting!"

Mr. Barlow laughed merrily and swung her into the dance. "Was it not? She retired to her hotel, sent for Kitty, and declared that if she really chose to marry an arrant mooncalf, she wished her joy of him."

"With such a mother, it is not surprising that Lord Peter has so little to say for himself."

"Poor fellow. Of course Kitty has no notion of being intimidated into holding her tongue. She up and said straight out to Lady Leighton that it wasn't Glossop's fault he fell in. She and Sir Nathan both distracted his attention at the wrong moment, she said. And her ladyship smiled and said, 'I believe you will do, young woman,' and invited Kitty and my mother to dine with her tonight."

"Gracious, it couldn't have worked out better if it had been plotted beforehand." Jessica was reminded of her own idea for a plot to bring Nathan and Lucy together.

Over Mr. Barlow's shoulder, she caught sight of Lord Alsop, who was to play a vital rôle in her plans. He was clad in crimson velvet and gold lace tonight. With the addition of a periwig, doubtless he would have cut a fine figure in an eighteenth century ballroom. In these modern times he bore a distressing resemblance to a footman in livery, except that no footman would be seen dead with padded shoulders and a pinched-in waist.

He was watching the entrance. Jessica followed his gaze and saw Nathan enter with Lucy, followed by

Tibby and Mrs. Woodcock. They must all have arrived at the same moment. She glanced quickly back at his lordship and noted his expression of mingled covetousness and resentment.

Most satisfactory. He hadn't the nerve to compete with Nathan, but he still wanted Lucy.

"I don't believe you have heard a word I said," complained Mr. Barlow good-naturedly.

"I beg your pardon, I was distracted by Lord Alsop's costume."

He grinned. "Fit for a fancy-dress ball, ain't he? A dunghill cock, all show, no go."

"Just what I was thinking. But I was attending to you, too, sir. You were telling me that you and Kitty are to have a double wedding. I wish you very happy."

Thus encouraged, Mr. Barlow continued to expound upon his plans, while Jessica silently devised the details of her own.

She managed matters so that at the end of the dance they were close to Lord Alsop.

"Good evening, my lord," she said with a smile.

Neither he nor Bob Barlow quite succeeded in hiding their surprise at her unwonted cordiality, but the baron was quick to take advantage.

"Do me the honour of standing up with me, ma'am," he requested suavely.

Since that was precisely what Jessica wanted, she did her best to conceal her distaste, though she doubted his lordship had sufficient sensibility to notice. Fortunately the next set was a country dance that would keep him at a distance most of the time.

"I am very glad the weather is improved, are not you?" she asked as they stood waiting for the music to begin.

"Constant rain does become oppressive," he agreed. "Nothing is pleasanter than to stroll in Sydney Gardens on a fine day with a fair lady on one's arm. Perhaps you..."

"I miss my drawing when it is wet," Jessica interrupted. "I prefer to sketch out of doors. How delightful was our picnic on Beechen Cliff—but I fear you found it tedious, sir. A ladies' sketching party can hold little amusement for a man of the world."

"On the contrary, ma'am, a man of the world such as myself is able to find something of interest in any company. In your company, of course, my dear Miss Franklin, one has not to seek far for entertainment."

As his gaze was glued to her bosom, she did not suppose for a moment that it was her sparkling conversation that held his attention. "I enjoy drawing buildings," she persevered.

"Bath is the ideal place to exercise your talents, ma'am." His insinuating voice hinted at a *double entendre*.

Jessica ignored it. "There are indeed many fine buildings here. I have not yet attempted the Royal Crescent."

"A magnificent curve," Lord Alsop leered.

"If the sun is shining, I mean to draw it tomorrow morning. The shadows will be just right at about ten o'clock, I believe. I shall invite Miss Pearson to accompany me, for it is useless to expect my brother's escort when all I shall do is sit and sketch." Lucy was unlikely to refuse to go with her, though sketching was hardly her favourite occupation.

The baron's cold eyes brightened with a calculating look. He had taken the bait.

She endured the country dance, wishing she could inform Nathan of what she was suffering for his sake. He and Lucy were in a nearby set. When the final chord sounded and Jessica had curtsied to Lord Alsop's bow, she slipped across to Lucy's side, took her arm, and hurried her from the floor.

"Quick," she whispered, "before his lordship has a chance to ask me for another dance. He was ogling me in the horridest way, and I fear he means to invite me to walk with him tomorrow."

"You need not accept. That is perfectly proper, not like refusing to stand up with a gentleman."

"But I shall refuse with more conviction if I can say that I have a prior engagement. Will you go with me to sketch the Royal Crescent? I have been longing for a chance at it."

Lucy's assent was notably lacking in enthusiasm.

Jessica's next partner was Nathan, who was inclined to haul her over the coals for dancing with Lord Alsop. She diverted him with the story of Kitty Barlow's triumph.

"She does well for herself," he said, "but they are truly fond of each other, I believe. I daresay Lady Leighton was right to grant her approval."

Jessica regarded this as a hopeful sign. The gulf between the son of a marquis and the daughter of a country squire was surely no less than that between a baronet and the daughter of a Cit. All her obstinate brother needed was a push in the right direction.

When next the figures of the dance brought them together, she said, "Lucy's such an obliging girl—she has offered to keep me company while I sketch the Royal Crescent tomorrow, but I fear she'll be sadly bored. Drawing is not a favoured pastime with her. If you're not otherwise engaged, could you happen to pass that way at, say, a quarter past ten, to keep her entertained for me? Otherwise I shall feel rushed and I shan't be able to do justice to a difficult subject."

"Purely by chance I just might happen to walk that way," he assured her, grinning.

Matthew was waiting for her when they returned to Miss Tibbett at the end of the set.

"I thought I should have to come and pry you out of the card room," she greeted him.

"I'm flattered to think you would even consider such an improper course rather than simply looking for another partner," he riposted. "But I did not stay long in the card room. I have been watching you and I want to know what you are up to."

"Up to?" Jessica tried to sound innocent, but cast a hasty glance at Miss Tibbett. "I don't know what you mean."

He took her arm and drew her to a pair of empty seats at a little distance. "First, you were unusually taciturn while dancing with Barlow."

"Mr. Barlow talks quite enough for two. I must tell you about Kitty."

"Later. Second, you stood up with Lord Alsop, though I know you to be perfectly capable of depressing his pretensions . . ."

"It is very rude to refuse to stand up with a gentleman."

". . . And you seemed to have no difficulty in finding words enough for him. In fact, it seemed to me that you approached him, rather than the other way about."

"I found myself near him. I could hardly cut him dead!"

Matthew grinned. "I don't see why not. He's too cowardly to call you out."

"Do you think so?" she asked eagerly. A duel was the one possibility she was worried about. "That is, too cowardly to issue a challenge to a gentleman?"

"So I believe. What *are* you plotting, Jessica?"

She ignored this impertinent question. "Mr. Barlow said he has as much pluck as a dunghill cock."

"Mr. Barlow had no business using farmyard language in your presence." He was openly laughing at her now.

"And I have no business repeating it. It is very shocking, to be sure, but somehow I don't think you are shocked."

"I doubt anything you could say to me would shock me, so just cut line and tell me what machinations have put that wicked sparkle in your eyes."

Jessica turned her head away to hide the wistfulness that drove the mischief from her eyes. How very much she wished she could believe he would not be shocked if—when—she revealed that she was not an heiress. She sniffed unhappily.

"Don't cry," said Matthew at once. "I didn't mean to upset you. Here." He thrust a handkerchief into her hand.

Jessica caught a glimpse of an embroidered rosebud in the corner before he seized it back and substituted another, a large, masculine square of fine, plain white linen. Any desire to sniff instantly departed, and she smiled to herself as she dabbed unnecessarily at her eyes.

Matthew turned the conversation to the betrothal of Kitty Barlow and Lord Peter Glossop, but he had no intention of leaving the matter there. For the next few days he meant to keep a close watch on Miss Jessica Franklin's every move. Whatever mischief she was up to, he would be there to save her from the consequences.

was no trouble to keep a close watch on Miss Jessica
Franklin's gray mare. Whatever mischief she was up
to, he would be there to save her from the consequences.

CHAPTER SEVENTEEN

"I WANT YOU TO KEEP an eye on Miss Pearson, Tad,"
said Jessica as she and the footman walked up Gay
Street, "but whatever happens, don't interfere unless I
call you."

"Right, Miss Jess." Tad looked mystified. "Er, what
exac'ly was you expecting to happen?"

"I'm sure I cannot guess," she told him blithely, satisfied with her precautions.

It was not yet ten o'clock when they arrived at the
Circus, but the day was already hot. Jessica felt a momentary qualm— Lucy, she recalled, did not care for
hot weather. Still, that was a minor discomfort, and
after all, the whole plot was for Lucy's sake as much as
Nathan's.

Lucy was waiting, delicately pretty in white muslin
with pale pink ruffles. Her sketching pad and pencils
appeared almost as untouched as the day they had been
purchased at a superior London shop. Tad added them
to his load and followed as the two young ladies strolled
along Brock Street, chatting about last night's assembly. They reached the beginning of the Royal Crescent
and paused to admire the splendid building, a sweep-
ing two-hundred-yard arc of Bath stone with Ionic columns framing the windows of the upper stories. On the
ledge at the foot of the columns, the inhabitants of

some of the houses had put out pots of pink or red geraniums, adding a touch of gaiety.

"The combination of curve and perspective is going to be a real challenge," said Jessica, nearly forgetting her plans in her enthusiasm. She turned and looked down the steep slope of lawn opposite the houses. Two men were at work with scythes, filling the air with the scent of new-mown grass. "I believe the best view will be from the far end. Shall we sit under that oak?" she suggested.

"Oh yes, the shade will be pleasant," Lucy agreed, so they walked the length of the crescent and settled under the tree.

Tad wandered off to pass the time of day with a maidservant who was scrubbing a doorstep, but he never took his eyes off the ladies for more than a moment, Jessica noted.

She gazed back along the crescent, planning her picture as if it were really the object of the outing. At the other end, too far off to make out the details, an open carriage and pair stood at the corner of Brock Street, the driver lounging at ease. She wished it would come closer so that she could incorporate it into her sketch.

Then she saw Lord Alsop coming towards them. All artistic considerations fled.

She jumped to her feet. "I believe I shall take a closer look at the details of the railings and the heads of the columns before I begin drawing," she said, and ignoring Lucy's faint protest, she started off across the grass to meet the baron.

He was wearing a green and white striped coat this morning; his white-topped boots had green tassels and he carried a green-lacquered cane. As Jessica approached, he swept off his top hat and bowed as deeply as his tailor's and his valet's work permitted.

"Well met, fair Jessica," he pronounced meaningfully, and offered her his arm. "Shall we walk a little?"

"I was just going to inspect the details of the columns, my lord."

"Ah yes, your drawing. An ingenious excuse for a rendezvous."

"Miss Pearson did agree to come with me, as I expected. She is sitting under that tree, waiting for me." Jessica indicated the solitary figure. Lucy had stood up and was peering anxiously in their direction. So was Tad, but she doubted whether Lord Alsop would recognize him as her servant at this distance.

"I doubt Miss Pearson will protest at a little dalliance," said his lordship. He grabbed Jessica, pressed her to his chest, and planted a wet kiss right on her lips.

Outraged, Jessica struggled, turning her head from his foul breath. This was not what was supposed to happen! The wretched baron had got it all wrong: he was meant to persecute Lucy with his unwanted attentions, not her.

He was stronger than he looked. She could not free herself, and he managed to drop another kiss on her right eyebrow. Then he staggered back as she hit him on the nose with the top of her head.

"Really, Miss Franklin," he gasped, tears starting in his eyes, "I like a girl with a bit of spirit, but this is taking things too..." His voice trailed away as he saw Nathan speeding up the hill with an expression that would have done credit to an avenging Fury.

Without wasting time on words, the outraged brother swung a right fist with all the power of youth and wrath behind it. Lord Alsop stretched his length on the grass.

"Get up so I can hit you again," Nathan snarled. The baron wisely made no move to obey. "I'll pick you up if I have to."

Jessica hung on to Nathan's arm. He had vastly exceeded the demands of his script, coming to the rescue as intended but with rather more enthusiasm than she had expected. A crowd was gathering, the two mowers panting up hill and a score of servants swarming down from the Crescent.

Miraculously, Matthew pushed through the crowd and put a restraining hand on Nathan's shoulder.

Lord Alsop raised his head cautiously and pointed an accusing finger at his attacker. "Assaulting a peer!" he screeched. "I'll see you transported for this. You are all witnesses." He gestured to the men with scythes. "You two, arrest him."

The mowers hesitated. The crowd was murmuring, and a man dressed as a groom stepped forward. "Best take 'im to the Guildhall," he advised. "The justice'll sort it out better nor we can."

"No!" cried Jessica. "He's my brother, he was only..."

"I'll willingly go before the magistrate," Nathan's militant voice interrupted. "Doubtless he'll have something to say about old lechers forcing themselves on innocent girls. Look after her, Walsingham, will you? Come on, fellows."

The groom helped the baron scramble to his feet as Nathan set off, marching down the hill with the scythers on either side of him. Half a dozen onlookers joined the escort while the others drifted away.

Jessica's head whirled. Matthew was there, supporting her. "Did the brute hurt you?" he asked anxiously. "I came as fast as I could, but this wretched leg of mine..."

"No, no, I'm all right," she cried. "But it's all my fault. I must go after them and explain."

"My curricle's just a step away, in Brock Street. I shall drive you down to the Guildhall. Was not Miss Pearson with you?"

"Yes, I had forgotten." Overwhelmed with guilt, Jessica looked around wildly. Lucy had disappeared, but so had Tad. "My footman is with her, she will be quite safe. Oh pray, let us go at once."

By the time the curricle reached Queen Square, Jessica had recovered her composure sufficiently to begin to wonder just how Matthew happened to be in the right place at the right time.

"What," she demanded, "was your business in Brock Street this morning?"

"I was keeping watch over a young lady whose eyes were bright with mischief last night."

"I've been wicked," said Jessica mournfully.

"Tell me."

The tale poured forth. "You see, Nathan is positively *bat-witted* about Mr. Pearson being a Cit, as though that could possibly matter when he and Lucy love each other. So I thought if I arranged for him to save her from Lord Alsop... I even hoped his lordship would kiss her. I didn't know it would be so utterly horrid, or I never would have done it. And then the wretched man was not the least bit interested in Lucy!" she ended on a note of indignation.

"I'd like to say that your manifest charms clearly outweigh Miss Pearson's, but I imagine it was rather a

case of a bird in the hand being worth two in the bush,"
said Matthew, laughing. "You must admit you appeared to give him every encouragement to believe you
willing."

"The toad! I am afraid that is what he will tell the
justice. Nathan couldn't really be transported, could
he?"

"I doubt it. He's landed gentry, after all, if not a no-
bleman, and whatever your part in the business, he had
provocation. Besides, Lord Alsop's reputation even
here in Bath is hardly spotless."

Jessica was sure his cheerfulness was forced, to reas-
sure her. Visions of her brother in chains on a convict
ship to Australia flitted through her head. Even if it
didn't come to that, a large fine or thirty days in prison
would ruin them. And it was all her fault. How could
she possibly have been such a knock-in-the-cradle?

The streets were busy by now, and the curricle made
slow progress. They reached the Guildhall just in time
to see Lord Alsop totter through the doors, supported
by a large footman in blue livery, one of the servants
who had taken French leave from the Royal Crescent.
As soon as Matthew's bays drew to a halt, Jessica
jumped down and hurried after them.

She found herself in a long, crowded room filled with
a murmur of voices. At the far end, behind a table on a
low platform, sat the justice of the peace, with his clerk
nearby on a high stool at a tall desk. Jessica thought she
recognized the magistrate, a small man with a surpris-
ingly loud voice. She heard someone address him as
"Alderman," and then someone else as "Mr. Perrin,
sir." He was the jeweller whose shop in Milsom Street
she patronized for her insignificant purchases.

The crowd seemed to have swallowed Nathan. She could see Lord Alsop's striped coat, but she had no desire to go anywhere near him. The room was divided by wooden barricades, and she didn't know which way to go.

She felt a hand on her arm and turned to find Matthew at her side.

"Oh dear," he said, surveying her ruefully. "I wonder if I have a comb in my pocket."

"I have one in my reticule."

The nearby members of the crowd watched indifferently as he removed her straw hat and tidied her hair. She shivered at his touch.

"Are you cold? A shawl would lend credibility to your claim to be a respectable young lady, but I fear there is nothing to be done about that now."

She replaced her hat; he straightened it and tied the yellow ribbons beneath her chin. Looking up into his grey eyes, she wondered at how warm a colour grey could be.

"Bound over to Assizes," boomed Alderman Perrin, and thumped with his gavel on the table.

"Next case," said the clerk in a bored voice, scribbling madly with his quill.

"I demand immediate justice," cried Lord Alsop. "I am a Peer of the Realm."

Mr. Perrin conferred with his clerk. The crowd shifted and parted as the baron and his escort pushed forward. Matthew took Jessica's hand and led her in their wake. His clasp was firm and reassuring. When they reached the last wooden railing, Nathan was already there, looking handsome, young, and full of righteous wrath. Lord Alsop was nearby, leaning feebly on the footman's arm as if he were at death's door.

"Name?" asked the clerk, still bored.

"Baron Alsop of Crowmoor."

"Chair for his lordship." There was a pause while an usher brought a chair and opened the barricade to let his lordship through. "Business?" queried the clerk.

"This impertinent young jackanapes assaulted me." He jabbed a finger at Nathan.

"Name?"

"Sir Nathan Franklin, Baronet, of Langdale."

"Chair for Sir Nathan."

"I'll stand. That aged lecher insulted my sister."

"Witnesses?"

There was a concerted murmur of "Aye, sir," "Here, sir," "That we be," from the servants and the mowers.

"I am a witness,'' said Jessica clearly. "I am Miss Jessica Franklin, Sir Nathan's sister."

"Chair for Miss Franklin."

"Pray be seated, Miss Franklin," said Mr. Perrin courteously.

Jessica didn't want to let go Matthew's hand, nor move away from his comforting presence, but the usher was opening the barricade. She went through and sat on the hard wooden chair, aware of craning necks and whispers in the crowd.

"I take it you don't deny striking his lordship, Sir Nathan?" asked the magistrate. Nathan shook his head. "Miss Franklin, perhaps you would kindly inform me, what...er...form did the alleged insult take?"

"The toad kissed me."

Someone sniggered loudly.

"My lord?" invited Mr. Perrin, casting on the baron a look of distaste.

"The jade set up a rendezvous," he claimed. "She'd have been happy enough to go along if her brother hadn't caught her at it."

"I happened to mention that I intended to sketch the Royal Crescent this morning," she retorted with spirit. "How was I to know that a so-called gentleman old enough to be my grandfather would regard that as an invitation to maul me?"

Mr. Perrin turned to Nathan. "It seems clear to me that you were provoked. However, to resort to violence against a peer is an offence against..." He hesitated as a door in the wall behind him swung open.

Mr. Pearson came in. Jessica caught a glimpse of Lucy's pink-ruffled gown to one side of the open door and then her face appeared, round eyes gazing anxiously after her father. He stumped up to his fellow-jeweller and engaged him in a low-voiced discussion of which Nathan and Lord Alsop, to judge by the glances sent their way, were the objects.

Then he nodded briskly, sent Jessica a wink and a grin, and returned to his daughter. The door closed behind him.

"Well, Sir Nathan," said the magistrate, "you have a highly respected character witness vouching for you. Ten shillings fine and bound over to keep the peace for one year. And you, my lord—forty shillings and bound over for a year. Disgraceful behaviour for a gentleman of your age." His gavel thumped twice.

"Next case," called the clerk, scratching madly with his pen and ignoring a babble of outrage from Lord Alsop.

The usher opened the barricade and Jessica sped to Matthew's side.

"Bless him!" she said softly. "And bless Lucy for fetching him. How can Nathan possibly hold out against that?"

"I don't know, but I shouldn't count on anything if I were you," he said.

She looked over to where her brother was paying his fine. In his face, jubilation warred with chagrin.

"You are right." She sighed. "I must talk to him. Thank you, sir, for...just for being there when I needed you."

She slipped away to join Nathan. When she glanced back, Matthew was still standing amid the crowd, watching her. His expression of yearning shook her to the core.

Neither brother nor sister was in the mood for conversation as they walked the short distance home to North Parade. Jessica thanked Nathan for saving her from the odious baron, and he grumbled at her in a perfunctory way for allowing herself to be caught in such a disgraceful situation. Then silence fell between them. When they reached Number 15, Nathan would have gone straight upstairs, but Jessica pulled him into the drawing room.

"Well?" she demanded.

"Well what?" He dropped into a chair by the empty grate and scowled up at her.

"Mr. Pearson saved your bacon."

"I know it. I shall have to write to him, and devilish difficult it's going to be expressing my gratitude without crawling."

"You *cannot* continue to hold it against Lucy that he is a Cit."

Nathan jumped up and stalked over to the window. His grip on the sill was white-knuckled as he rested his forehead against the pane.

"I love her, Jess. And Mr. Pearson's a good sort. But in a way that makes it worse."

"Worse?"

"How can I go to him and say, 'I want to marry your daughter and I'm in urgent need of funds for Langdale?'"

"How can you let pride stand in the way of love? Think how you will hurt Lucy."

"Why should she believe I love her? She will have every justification for thinking I only want her money, and what can hurt her more than that?"

"I am persuaded that you wrong her. Whatever her father's considerations, she has never cared a pin for your title or your supposed wealth. She loves *you*, Nathan. She trusts you, she is comfortable with you as she is with few others. Perhaps Mr. Pearson will throw you out on your ear, but you must at least try to win her hand."

"I cannot!" he cried, swinging round, then added morosely, "I had best re-enlist, or go back to America and see if I can make a living there."

"Will you really be so poor-spirited as to give up Langdale without a fight and to leave me in the lurch into the bargain?"

"It's hopeless trying to save Langdale. Matthew will marry you, I don't doubt, but I don't expect you to ask him for the lease as a bride-gift."

"That's just as well, because Matthew has not a penny to his name."

That announcement broke through Nathan's preoccupation with his own emotions.

"What? He's old Stone's heir."

"Not any longer. He has been disinherited."

"Are you sure? How long have you known? Why did you not tell me?"

"I'm sure. I've known for several weeks. And there seemed no point in telling you and spoiling a fine friendship."

"Then Walsingham's a fortune hunter? I cannot believe it! And he dares to address you—I shall call him out."

"Don't be ridiculous."

Nathan glared at her, then his shoulders slumped. "You're right," he said dully. "He is no worse than I am." With a look of despair, he rushed from the room.

Jessica waited, tense, for the slam of the front door. Instead she heard his footsteps on the stair. Like an injured animal, he had retired to his den to lick his wounds.

It was all her fault, she thought hopelessly. Coming to Bath in search of wealthy spouses was her idea, and Nathan was her unwilling victim. Never again would she stoop to deceit.

CHAPTER EIGHTEEN

MATTHEW DIDN'T WANT Jessica to think he was following her, so when he left the Guildhall he drove to the York House Hotel. Lord Ilfracombe was just finishing his breakfast. Pulling out his watch, Matthew discovered it was not yet noon.

"Coffee?" offered his lordship hospitably. He was looking very pleased with himself. "Or would you prefer ale?"

"Ale, thank you, sir. It's been a long morning."

"Then you had better have some of this excellent cold sirloin. Waiter, bring some more muffins, if you please."

Having skimped on his own breakfast while watching for Jessica to pass his window, Matthew was glad to accept. He wolfed down the food, the earl looking on indulgently while sipping his coffee.

The secretary brought in some letters to be signed, then went out on an errand. Matthew finished his meal and sat back with a satisfied sigh. The efficient hotel waiters swiftly cleared the table and took themselves off.

"I don't mean to be inhospitable," said Lord Ilfracombe, "but I shall be leaving shortly for Stone Gables. Do I owe the honour of this visit to any particular business?"

"Yes." Matthew got up and began to pace restlessly. "I can't wait much longer, sir. Jessica—Miss Franklin—needs me, and lord knows I want her. Does my uncle show no signs of softening towards me?''

"Not precisely. He has reached a sort of *modus vivendi* with your cousin, I fear. That is, he manages to avoid him save at the dinner table.''

"Don't tell me Uncle Horace is content to have to dodge and hide in his own house!''

"To tell the truth, I have seen little of him.''

Matthew leaned with both hands on the table, frowning. "He was always a sociable man, by no means a recluse. Is he ill?''

"I think not." His lordship appeared to come to a decision. "You know, Matthew, I was going to advise you to wait a little longer, until he begins to feel the loss of . . . well, no matter. . . . But I believe the time may be ripe, after all. As you say, he must be thoroughly uncomfortable having to evade Biggin all the time. If you arrive with a wealthy bride on your arm, thus proving that you understand the value of money, I shouldn't be surprised if he forgave all and reinstated you as his heir.''

"Then Jessica need never know the whole, or at least not until we are safely wed. You, sir, as a dedicated bachelor, cannot understand how I long to make her mine.''

Astonishingly, the earl flushed. "As to that, I . . . er . . . I fear I have been practising a little deception of my own. My visits to Stone Gables have not been all on your behalf, nor is my advice to you to go there now entirely disinterested. Though I believe it's good advice,'' he added hastily.

"I certainly hope so!''

"You see, it has occurred to me that the return of the Prodigal Nephew might be just the thing to distract

Lord Stone when I tell him that he's going to lose his sister. I've persuaded Miss Stone to marry me.''

"Aunt Caroline! Good gad, sir, do you mean it? Then you *have* been wearing the willow for her all these years.''

"You must think me a shocking slowtop.''

"Well, if Jessica decided to devote her life to Nathan, I'd pester her half to death before I'd give up,'' Matthew vowed. "And if I couldn't make her change her mind then and there, I wouldn't go away for years and years, I'd haunt her every step and keep hoping.''

"I have wasted many years,'' Lord Ilfracombe admitted sadly.

"Then don't waste any more. Are you going to break the news to my uncle today?''

"Such is our intention. I shall ride over there as soon as I have rid myself of you.''

"Splendid.'' Matthew grinned. "I am going to ask Jessica to go for a drive in the country and we shall follow you.'' He leaned across the table and shook hands with the earl. "My congratulations, sir. No one could better deserve to win my Aunt Caro.''

Matthew's elation lasted until he had retrieved his curricle and his bays from the inn yard and turned the horses' heads towards North Parade. That was when he realized that in fact nothing had changed. There was no guarantee that Uncle Horace would welcome his return just because he was losing Caroline, nor that he would forgive his errant nephew because he was betrothed to an heiress.

If Matthew confessed to Jessica before he proposed, she would turn from him in scorn. In that case, being reinstated in his uncle's favour would mean nothing to him. But if he didn't confess and then Uncle Horace refused to relent, the fat would be well and truly in the fire.

He had come to no decision by the time he reached Number 15. Jessica and Miss Tibbett were in the drawing room; of Nathan there was no sign. Jessica's glad acceptance of his invitation cheered him somewhat.

"I must change for a drive in the country," she said, looking down at her daisy-sprigged muslin. "I shan't keep you above ten minutes."

She rushed off. He had noticed that her eyes were slightly red-rimmed and he guessed her brother's recalcitrance about Mr. Pearson to be the cause. What ailed Nathan to allow so small a matter to keep him from the girl he loved? Matthew was ready to spend the rest of his life striving to keep the smile in Jessica's hazel eyes— but it was all too likely that instead he was going to upset her further.

Miss Tibbett was regarding him gravely over her spectacles, and he had a sudden urge to ask her advice. He suppressed it; if she knew the truth she might forbid Jessica to drive with him.

"With your permission, ma'am," he said instead, "I should like to take Miss Franklin to see Stone Gables. It is some fifteen miles hence, so we shall be gone all afternoon."

"I see no reason why you should not," she acquiesced, "provided, of course, that your groom is with you?"

"Oh . . . yes, of course. I left him at home this morning. May I send your footman to fetch him?"

Tad was duly dispatched, and returned with Hanson just as Jessica came down. She was wearing a russet carriage dress that somehow made her hair look more like spun moonbeams than ever. All trace of tears was gone, doubtless banished by an application of cold water. She smiled at Matthew and his heart went out to her.

Nonetheless he was far from happy as he handed her into the curricle. As if he had not problems enough, how the devil was he to propose to her at all with the groom sitting up behind?

FROM HIS CHAMBER WINDOW, Nathan watched the smart vehicle with its superb bays set out down North Parade. Guilt left no room for envy in his mind. His pride was hurting Jess as well as Lucy, and—he had to admit it at last—himself.

When he thought of Lucy, all he wanted was to fold her gently in his arms and keep her safe from the world. And yet he was the one who caused her heartache.

It didn't bear thinking of. Suddenly making up his mind, he grabbed his hat and gloves, dashed down the stairs, and set off at a rapid stride for the upper part of town. If Mr. Pearson threw him out on hearing his story, at least Lucy would know he loved her and had tried to win her hand.

Reaching the Circus, he marched up to the door of the Pearsons' house as if he were going into battle, and knocked loudly. The haughty butler opened the door.

"I'd like a private word with Mr. Pearson," Nathan informed him.

Though Nathan had often escorted Lucy to and from the house, he had never, to the butler's knowledge, set eyes on its owner. But not by the quiver of an eyelid did that worthy indicate that he thought this request unusual.

"I shall see if Mr. Pearson is at home, sir," he said in a measured tone and went into the sitting room, closing the door behind him.

Lucy found the man intimidating, Nathan knew. She much preferred old Hayes, with his sagging wrinkles and his friendly manner that put her at ease. How she would enjoy living at Langdale among servants who would love her for their master's sake as well as for her gentle nature. He must have a new flower garden made for her in a sheltered spot; Jessica would know the best place.

His daydream shattered as the door of the sitting-room opened and a short, lean, elderly man—the man Nathan had seen at the Guildhall—came out into the hall.

"Good day, Sir Nathan." His handshake was warm and firm, and the shrewd look in his eye seemed not unfriendly—but of course that would change when he learned the worst. "Come into my study," he went on, leading the way across the hall, "though office'd be a better name for it. I like to keep my finger in the pie, don't you know, though officially I'm retired from the business."

As Jessica had said, he appeared to be a civil, respectable fellow. Any attempt to ape the refinement of a gentleman, or to toad-eat, would have set Nathan's back up at once, but he found nothing to cavil at. Mr. Pearson's clothes were well-made and of good quality, but by no means in the first stare of fashion. He looked and acted, in fact, like a sober, honest, and successful citizen.

"Sit down, sit down," he said, waving Nathan to a deep leather armchair. He himself took his seat behind a wide desk piled with several neat stacks of papers, and

Nathan decided on the straight chair in front of the desk. Somehow confession would be more difficult from the depths of an easy chair.

The butler brought in a tray with a bottle and two glasses. Nathan accepted a glass of Malaga but set the sweet wine untouched on the desk.

"Well, my boy?" said Mr. Pearson as the butler departed.

There was something excessively comforting about being called "my boy." Nathan was suddenly aware of how much he had missed his father, and he desperately wanted Mr. Pearson's liking and approval. He was about to forfeit both.

He put off the evil moment. "I want to thank you, sir, for coming to the rescue at the magistrate's court this morning."

"Why, it might just as well have been my Lucy yon fine gentleman was pawing, and I don't suppose you'd have held your punches if it was. She's told me often enough how you've kept the baron away. Miss Franklin hasn't taken any harm from his attentions, I hope?"

"No, Jessica can take care of herself. She had already hit him on the nose before I arrived."

"So Lucy told me. I'd've spoken to Jack Perrin the sooner if I hadn't been enjoying the way your sister laid into that rogue. Toad, she called him to his face." He chortled. "A mettlesome young lady, Miss Franklin."

Too mettlesome for him, Nathan acknowledged to himself. He had allowed her bold spirit to lead him into this bumblebath. "Jess is the best sister a fellow could ask for," he said loyally, "but it's a different sort of female I'm looking for. I want to marry your daughter, sir."

"Well, now." Mr. Pearson's eyes were bright and considering. "I'll not deny I've been expecting as much."

"There is something I must tell you before I ask your permission to address her," Nathan rushed on. "I daresay Miss Pearson has told you about Langdale?"

"To be sure. Not that it's ever crossed her mind, bless her heart, to wonder about your circumstances, but you're known in Bath as a wealthy landowner."

Nathan stared at his hands. "That's just it, sir, I'm not. The Franklins have held Langdale for centuries but we have never owned it. The lease is up at Michaelmas and I can't afford to renew it, at least not without selling all the sheep, and then there would be nothing to farm." He looked up at his beloved's father, whose face was inscrutable. "I'll leave at once, sir, if you wish, but though I realize you won't find it easy to believe, I really do love Lucy."

"Oh, I believe it, my boy. If you didn't, I doubt you'd have troubled yourself to confess as yet, for once Lucy had accepted you I'd have had the devil of a time pulling her out of it. She'd take you if you was a pauper."

"Do you think so, sir?" His heart warmed. "It's not quite that bad, but I shan't have enough to support a family in comfort."

"I'm right glad you've got the courage to tell me."

Jumping to his feet, Nathan flared up. "I give no one leave to doubt my courage!"

"Nay, lad, I'm not calling you a coward, but there's different kinds of bravery. There's facing the enemy's guns—I don't doubt you've won your spurs. And there's facing your own faults and weaknesses, which is more difficult. And then there's admitting to someone

whose good opinion you need that you've been trying
to deceive them...well, that may be the hardest of all.''

"Trying to...but you said...Jess said..."

"...That I'd welcome you for a son-in-law? That was
my own little bit o' prevarication, like. If you'd come
asking me for my girl and hadn't confessed to being a
fortune hunter, I'd've sent you to the rightabout and
told you Miss Franklin must've misunderstood.''

"Then you knew all along!" Nathan was bewil-
dered.

"I may know naught o' sheep, my boy, but I can tell
you fools don't prosper in the City. The moment you
started making eyes at Lucy I sent a man up north to
find out what he could about Sir Nathan Franklin,
Baronet, and I can tell you I wasn't pleased with what
he told me.''

"Who can blame you," said Nathan gloomily.

"Then your sister brought back the bracelet I gave
her—nice and polite as you please, but firm with it.
Worth a pretty penny, it was, and that gave me pause. I
can tell you, if I was thirty years younger I'd be proposing to Mistress Jessica myself,'' he admitted with a
cheerful wink. "I wouldn't be surprised if this whole
fortune-hunting business was her notion, but I like you
the better for not blaming the deception on her.''

"Does Miss Pearson know?"

"Not from me, she don't. I'll leave you to tell her."

"I will, sir, I promise." He hesitated, incredulous of
the implications. "You mean you don't object to my
asking for her hand?''

"I don't mind telling you, my boy, I'll be right put
out if you don't after all the trouble I've been to.''

"Trouble?"

"That man Scunthwaite's a hard man to deal with, no mistake, and not knowing aught of sheep didn't make it any easier, though it's my belief he thinks there's coal at Langdale."

"You have already bought the lease!"

"Nay, lad, anyone in the City can tell you Ben Pearson likes to own what he owns. I've bought up Langdale, every last stone and blade of grass of the place, and the coal underneath if any there be. You'll get the lease as a marriage settlement, and the deed's going to be a christening present for my first grandson."

"I don't know what to say, sir." Nathan leant across the desk and heartily shook his future father-in-law's hand. "Except that I'll make her happy, I swear I will."

"Well, now, you can't say fairer than that." Mr. Pearson regarded him with beaming indulgence. "You'd best be off and tell her so. She's in the room across the hall."

Nathan lost no time in obeying. When he opened the door of the sitting room, she was standing with bowed head by a table in the window. Her dainty figure, in white with blue ribbons, was taut with a tension that surely had nothing to do with the *Ladies' Magazine* lying open before her.

"Lucy?" he said.

She turned and ran into his arms. Neither of them heard Mrs. Woodcock tut-tutting.

"Kissing before they are even properly betrothed!" scolded that scandalized lady as Mr. Pearson, grinning, quietly removed her from the room.

CHAPTER NINETEEN

IT WAS A PERFECT afternoon for a drive in the country. A cooling breeze had broken the morning's promise of heat. Breathing the mingled scent of honeysuckle and dog rose, Jessica made a determined effort to put her unhappiness behind her.

"Are we going to Prior Park?" she asked, as Matthew took the south-west road out of Bath. "I have heard that it is well worth a visit."

"Have you not yet visited it? I shall have to remedy that one of these days, but no, not today, though we shall pass close by. I want…that is, I hope to show you Stone Gables."

"Your uncle's house?" She was astonished.

"Yes. You don't think it too far? It's fifteen miles or so, but I have your aunt's permission."

"I'd love to see it." Was she wrong about him after all? Had she too quickly believed Tad's report of his disinheritance? Surely he would not take her to see Lord Stone if he had quarrelled with him irrevocably.

While she was trying to think of a delicate way to probe for answers, particularly difficult with the groom hearing every word, Matthew quickly changed the subject. The road ran uphill alongside a pair of metal tracks, and he explained how Ralph Allen had re-opened the ancient quarries at Combe Down and built the railway to carry Bath stone down to the growing town.

"John Wood the Elder was designing and building Queen Square and the Parades and the Circus at the time, eighty years ago. Allen made a fortune from the stone and had Wood design Prior Park for him. You'll see it in a minute, when we pass these trees."

Jessica gasped at the sight. Spread across the top of the hill, with a view down to Bath, Prior Park was a vast mansion in the grandest Palladian style. On each side of a central block with huge Corinthian columns, a curving arcade of arches led to symmetrical wings.

"An architect's dream, isn't it?" said Matthew cheerfully, amused at her awe. "All you need is a patron with money and vision, and a perfect site, and a nearby quarry full of beautiful stone. I suppose you want to draw it?"

"Oh yes, one day, if I can find paper large enough."

"I'll find you some," he promised, laughing. "Mr. Allen didn't disdain the simpler side of life, either. He built some excellent cottages for his quarry workers in the village. We'll drive past those, too."

They continued to discuss architecture for the next several miles, but Matthew seemed to grow more and more uneasy. At last he lapsed into silence, concentrating on driving through the narrow, twisting lanes. The hedgerows were abloom with ragged robin, Queen Anne's lace, purple foxgloves and yellow toadflax, but Jessica found it impossible to appreciate their beauty.

The longer the silence between them went on, the more difficult it became to speak. She felt an almost tangible tension, full of indecipherable meaning. Possibilities flitted through her head.

She was right about the break with his uncle, she was sure of it. Matthew meant to show her Stone Gables the way he had shown her Prior Park, driving past for a torturing glimpse of what he had lost. Or perhaps he had found out that Lord Stone was away from home. He would take her to call on Miss Stone—he was very fond of his aunt—and then, having waved the carrot before her, he would propose.

Was he going to confess to his deception? If he didn't, did it mean there was nothing to confess? In that case, how was she going to reveal her own lack of fortune? How could she ask him for the Langdale lease as a bride-gift? Why, oh why, had she ever come up with the baconbrained notion of going to Bath to seek a rich husband?

She must have been mad, she thought miserably.

The bays slowed, pulling the curricle up a hill. On one side of the lane was a wall, with a wood beyond it. They came to a white-painted gate leading to a grassy ride between the trees, and Matthew reined in his pair.

Hanson jumped down and opened the gate.

"This is where you start walking," Matthew told him as he drove through.

"Aye, sir," said the groom philosophically. "'Tain't no more nor a mile." He saluted, closed the gate, and set off along a path through the wood.

"You don't mind, do you?" Matthew asked Jessica. "We're on my uncle's land now. I doubt if even Miss Tibbett would object."

"I cannot speak for Aunt Tibby, but I don't mind," she said with a certain caution.

They continued up the ride in the cool shade of oaks and sycamores. The woods were well cared for, clear of underbrush, with stacks of fresh-cut timber now and then showing that old trees were regularly felled. Somewhere a jay screeched a warning and a cock pheasant dashed across in front of the carriage. On the grass the horses' hooves and the wheels were silent; the twittering of birds filled the air, punctuated by a knocking woodpecker.

Jessica looked at Matthew. His face was set, unreadable.

They emerged from the woods into sunshine, reached the top of the rise, and stopped. Before them parkland dotted with oaks spread down to a stream, then rose again. Half way up the opposite slope sprawled Stone Gables.

"That's what happens when half a dozen builders over the course of three centuries get their hands on a house," said Matthew. "The original manor is Tudor, but every Viscount Stone since has added his own pile of stones in the current style."

"I like it," she assured him. "It may not be as grand as Prior Park but it looks far more comfortable. At least every architect seems to have added a few more gables to unify the design."

His smile was strained and he turned quickly back to the view. "I like it, too. I thought it would be mine one day. Miss Franklin, I cannot bear to deceive you any longer. I was my uncle's heir but he disinherited me before ever I met you. I am no better than a common fortune hunter."

"I know," said Jessica simply.

"You know!" He stared at her, hope dawning. "And you still . . . Then you . . ."

"Wait." Taken by surprise, she still hadn't found the right words. Perhaps there were no right words. "I have no expectations, either. We never owned Langdale and we can't afford to renew the lease. When the stock is sold I'll have a little money, maybe enough to rent a cottage in the country, but that is all. Barely enough to live on." Desolate, she dashed away the tears that blurred her vision.

Matthew dropped the reins and took her in his arms. "Don't cry, Jess." His voice was urgent. "Marry me anyway. I have a small income from my father, we'll get by. Jessica, my darling, I love you. Nothing else matters." Knocking her hat askew, he kissed her brimming eyes.

She clung to him. "Do you mean it?"

"I've loved you, I think, since I caught you looking back at me your first day in North Parade."

Her tears vanished as she read the teasing warmth in his gaze. "And I was so afraid you'd believe me a brazen hussy."

"Oh, I did."

It was not the moment to contradict him, so she kissed him to prove him right. He seemed to appreciate the confirmation.

Some time later, the horses shifted restlessly. Jessica emerged from the embrace, pink-cheeked and dishevelled, and rescued her hat, which was slipping down the back of her neck, in imminent danger of permanent damage from two strong arms. She set it carefully on the curricle's floor so as not to discourage any further assaults upon her dignity. Matthew calmed his bays.

"You will marry me, won't you? I know I haven't asked you properly but it's difficult to go down on one knee in an open vehicle."

"You cannot suppose that I would pass up the chance to have a famous architect for a husband. We shall only be poor for a little while, until you have made your mark."

"With you help, my beloved artist, I will," he vowed, kissing her again but with one wary eye on the horses. "I think we had best go on down before they decide to drop us in the stream on the way to the stables. Where's my comb got to?"

For the second time that day he tidied her hair and adjusted her hat. It took considerably longer this time, as he had created far more havoc than Lord Alsop, and besides, it was far more enjoyable putting it to rights in private than in a crowded courtroom. One of the horses neighed impatiently.

Pinker-cheeked than ever, and feeling strangely weak, Jessica adjusted the bow beneath her chin as Matthew drove down the hill.

"Are you going to introduce me to Lord Stone?" she asked uncertainly. "Or is he from home? I should like to meet your aunt."

"I want to present you to both of them. Lord Ilfracombe suggested that my uncle might relent if I turned up with a rich bride. He has an excessive regard for money."

"But I'm not rich."

"That will not matter if Uncle Horace thinks you are."

"Oh no, Matthew, no more pretending. I don't mean to tell even the smallest taradiddle ever again."

"You're right, of course." Smiling wryly, he reached out with one hand and touched her cheek. "I don't believe I'm more of a liar than the next man, but after being caught up in this hoax for the last few months I'm going to need you to be my conscience for a while."

"Oh dear!" Jessica laughed unsteadily. "Not a very good one, I fear."

"An irresistible one."

Crossing the stream by a narrow arch of stone, they joined the avenue leading from the park's main entrance to the house and moments later pulled up before the front door. Hanson had beaten them to it and was waiting with a knowing look to take the curricle round to the stables.

The door stood welcomingly open on that warm afternoon, a good omen, Jessica hoped. She was too anxious to gain more than a vague impression of a large, airy hall, panelled in dark wood, with a gallery at one end. A butler was lurking—that was the only possible word for it—near the open door to a room on their right, from which came voices. He saw them and moved forward to meet them.

"Mr. Matthew! It's good to see you, sir."

"A fine afternoon, Bristow. This is Miss Franklin."

Jessica nodded and smiled in answer to the butler's bow, but she was more interested in the roar of fury now emanating from the inner room. She clutched Matthew's arm.

"His lordship is in something of a testy mood, I fear," said Bristow.

They all stood there straining their ears.

"If you think I'll stand for a Dissenter inheriting Stone Gables, you've got even less sense in your cockloft than I gave you credit for."

The irate bellow was answered by a high-pitched voice. ("Cousin Archibald," murmured Matthew.) "I assure you, Uncle, the Anglican Church is following the Papists into the Great Pit..."

"I'd rather leave the place as a home for the widows of clergymen in reduced circumstances. If the Established Church ain't good enough for you, out with you! Out! Out!"

The sound of footsteps made Bristow move hastily away and assume an air of unconcern, but Matthew watched with undisguised interest and Jessica couldn't have torn her gaze from the open door if she had tried.

A tall, narrow-shouldered figure appeared, clad all in black, scuttling backwards on two spindly shanks.

"Cousin Archibald," Matthew murmured again.

Chasing Mr. Biggin came a small gentleman with white hair and a purple face. "Out! Out!" he repeated wrathfully. "Begone with you, sirrah! I'll have no brimstone preachers here."

Lord Ilfracombe appeared next, accompanied by a pretty woman who must, Jessica thought, be Matthew's Aunt Caroline. They stood at the doorway watching Lord Stone berate his alarmed nephew. Miss Stone looked worried, Lord Ilfracombe amused.

At that moment the viscount caught sight of Matthew.

"What the devil are *you* doing here?" he spluttered.

Mr. Biggin seized his chance to hurry up the stairs. Miss Stone swung round and started towards Matthew and Jessica, but Lord Ilfracombe put a hand on her arm to stop her.

Matthew took Jessica's hand and led her forward, quaking in her shoes.

"I thought it only proper, sir, to present my betrothed to the head of the family," he said blandly. "Miss Franklin has done me the honour of consenting to become my wife."

Jessica curtsied, taking heart as Lord Stone stared at her with more curiosity than displeasure. She was glad she had worn her new russet cambric, which became her admirably, and very glad that Matthew had tidied her hair.

The purple began to ebb from his cheeks. "Happy to make your acquaintance, Miss Franklin," he said with perfunctory courtesy, then turned back to Matthew. "So you've caught yourself an heiress, my boy?"

"Really, Horace!" Miss Stone intervened, breaking away from Lord Ilfracombe's restraint. "That is no way to speak of Matthew's intended. My dear Miss Franklin, I am so very delighted to meet you and to welcome you to Stone Gables."

"Thank you, Aunt Caro," said Matthew as Jessica curtsied again, warming at once to her kindly greeting.

"Thank you, ma'am. I am happy to meet Mr. Walsingham's favourite aunt." Gathering all her courage, she turned back to his lordship to answer the query he had addressed to Matthew. "I fear, my lord, I am no heiress."

"That's not to say, Uncle, that I was aware of Miss Franklin's...er, reduced circumstances until very recently." Matthew looked down at her with fond possessiveness.

The viscount let out a brief cackle.

Emboldened by the lack of a fearsome rebuke, Jessica went on, "I was in Bath seeking a wealthy husband, you see, and I thought I had found one. I was quite taken in."

"Two fortune hunters in pursuit of each other!" Lord Stone positively chortled with glee. "Sounds like something out of a Restoration comedy, don't it, Caroline? I suppose, miss, since you discovered my nephew has no expectations, you are ready to release him from his promise?"

"Oh no, sir!" Matthew put his arm around her waist as if he was afraid she might run away. "Jessica knew the worst before she accepted my hand, and as for me, I fear your effort to teach me the value of money has failed. I am quite determined upon marrying her, for richer, for poorer, as the church says."

"Ha!" snorted his lordship, with a malevolent glare at the staircase up which his other nephew had recently vanished. "Bristow, send for my lawyer."

"And tea, Bristow," Miss Stone added hastily. "Miss Franklin, pray come up to my chamber and put off your hat."

"Wait," commanded her brother. He regarded Matthew and Jessica with bright eyes from which the tears of merriment had not yet quite vanished. "I don't *want* to leave Stone Gables to impoverished widows, however deserving." He gave a martyred sigh and went on in a grumbling tone, "I suppose you had best have the Bath house for the nonce, but I hope you will see fit to spend enough time here to learn to manage your inheritance, and to visit a lonely old man."

He cast a malicious glance at Miss Stone but, astounded by his words, Jessica scarcely noticed. She curtsied and murmured a few words of gratitude, then impulsively stepped forward and kissed his lordship's wrinkled cheek.

"Of course we shall visit you often, sir," she promised.

Looking pleased, he winked at Matthew and clapped him on the back. "I'd say you've got yourself a rare handful there, my boy."

"Jessica don't lack for audacity," Matthew agreed, laughing as he shook hands with his uncle. Lord Ilfracombe added amused congratulations, and Jessica was whisked away by Miss Stone before she could voice her indignation.

As they climbed the carved oak stair, darkened by centuries of use, Matthew's voice followed her: "You see, Uncle Horace, a milk-and-water miss wouldn't suit me at all."

She glanced back. He was watching her, so she blew him a kiss, then blushed and hurried after Miss Stone as the other two gentlemen looked up.

"A captivating young lady," said the viscount. "We'll open a bottle of the best to drink her health."

Miss Stone ushered Jessica into a large bedchamber comfortably furnished in ivory and blue. "You appear to have won my brother's approval, Miss Franklin," she said with a smile. "I hope you will come to like him. He is really the kindest of men, and only grows snappish when he is sorely tried."

Judging by what she had heard, Jessica considered "snappish" to be something of an understatement. She wanted to ask what had tried Lord Stone's temper so sorely today, but decided it would be impertinent to ask. Taking off her hat, she said, "I certainly cannot complain of his lordship's conduct, ma'am. He has been all that is obliging when he might reasonably have forbidden Mr. Walsingham to marry me. I fear you must think my deception very shocking."

"It is not for me to cavil at it, when I was aware in advance of Matthew's plans. Besides, since Ilfracombe first spoke of you I have been hoping that you and Matthew might make a match of it."

"Lord Ilfracombe told you about me?" she asked in surprise.

Miss Stone's cheeks grew pink. "We knew each other many years ago, and...and his lordship and I are betrothed," she confided.

"Oh, that is splendid news! He is an admirable gentleman. I wish you very happy, ma'am."

"I fear Horace was not pleased at the news. He looked sadly dismayed and I felt quite guilty about leaving him. And then my nephew Archibald made the mistake of declaring that the Anglican marriage service is rife with Romish practices. When he revealed that he has left the English Church...well, you heard the resultant discord. Horace is a strong proponent of the Established Church, and the owner of Stone Gables has three livings in his gift."

Jessica decided the viscount had had sufficient reason to disinherit Archibald Biggin. For the first time, she wondered why Matthew had been banished. "What mistake did Mr. Walsingham make?" she asked tentatively.

"Oh dear, I'm not sure...but if I do not tell you, you will only imagine the worst. He pushed a young female—not, I'm afraid, a respectable female—down Bond Street in a wheelbarrow."

"A young female?" Jessica felt a sinking sensation in the pit of her stomach. "You mean, his...his...?"

"There, I knew I should not have told you." Miss Stone took both her hands. "My dear, Matthew went through a very difficult time when he was sent home from the Peninsula. He was confined to his bed, in great pain, for many months, and when he recovered enough to go about, he indulged in all sorts of youthful pranks. You see, when other young gentlemen of his age were let loose on the Town, he was fighting for his country. He does not speak of it, but I know it was very dreadful."

"He has talked to me about it, a little."

"That confirms my opinion, and Lord Ilfracombe's, that he is putting it behind him at last. Matthew has a great deal of common sense at bottom, and he was always a loving child. I do not think, my dear Miss Franklin, that you will regret becoming his wife."

"I love him," Jessica said, her shortlived doubts vanishing. "In the end, that's all that matters, isn't it?"

"It is, and I wish I had known that a dozen years ago." Miss Stone gave Jessica a quick hug and they went down to tea.

Lord Stone had completely recovered from his pique. When the ladies entered the drawing room, he rose with alacrity, made Jessica sit beside him, and fussed about her tea being exactly as she liked it. They discussed the amusements of Bath. Feeling more and more at home with him, she told him about the canal trip and he roared with laughter. They were fast friends by the time she and Matthew had to leave for the drive home.

"He asked me to call him uncle," she said to Matthew, waving one last time as they set off down the avenue with the groom up behind. "I like him, and your aunt is a dear."

"Yes, Aunt Caroline... Lord, I'd quite forgot your aunt—no, you said she is some sort of cousin. Must I ask Miss Tibbett's permission to marry you? And Jess, hasn't *she* got a fortune? Don't tell me she's disinherited you, to leave her money for the excavation of Roman ruins?"

"Tibby hasn't any money. As a matter of fact, she's not only not my aunt, she isn't even my cousin. She used to be my governess."

The moment of stunned silence was broken by a muffled guffaw from Hanson, then Matthew's shout of laughter made his startled horses toss their heads.

"At least my aunt is the real thing," he said, controlling the bays with practised ease, "and my uncle, too."

"Do you think he really would have left Stone Gables to the widows of clergy? It's hard to believe he was going to cut you off without a penny."

"As to that, he admitted while you were above stairs that though he did indeed change his will to leave Stone Gables to Cousin Archibald, he had still left me enough to live on comfortably. And he means to give us the North Parade house, not just let us live in it."

"How very kind, but I hope he will not change his mind yet again. Perhaps you had best not abandon architecture."

"I'd like to continue with it. You wouldn't mind? I should only accept commissions to design the most splendid mansions."

He sounded anxious for her approval. Jessica moved a little closer to him on the blue leather seat and said with all her love in her voice, "As far as I'm concerned, Matthew darling, you can design pigsties. I shall just have to learn to draw pigs."

He looked down at her with a grin that quickly changed to something warmer. Halting the horses, he pulled her into his arms.

When they drove on, he drove slowly, the reins held in his right hand and his left arm about her waist. Hanson sighed. It was going to be a long journey home.

Back by Popular Demand

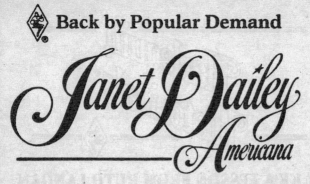

Janet Dailey
Americana

A romantic tour of America through fifty favorite
Harlequin Presents, each set in a different state
researched by Janet and her husband, Bill. A journey
of a lifetime in one cherished collection.

In January, don't miss the exciting states featured in:

Title #23 **MINNESOTA**
            Giant of Mesabi

     #24 **MISSISSIPPI**
           A Tradition of Pride

**Available wherever
Harlequin books are sold.**

TAKE A LESSON FROM RUTH LANGAN, BRONWYN WILLIAMS, LYNDA TRENT AND MARIANNE WILLMAN...

A *history* lesson! These and many more of your favorite authors are waiting to sweep you into the world of conquistadors and countesses, pioneers and pirates. In Harlequin Historicals, you'll rediscover the romance of the past, from the Great Crusades to the days of the Gibson girls, with four exciting, sensuous stories each month.

So pick up a Harlequin Historical and travel back in time with some of the best writers in romance.... Don't let history pass you by!

Harlequin Intrigue®

43 Light St.

It looks like a charming old building near the Baltimore waterfront, but inside 43 Light Street lurks danger...and romance.

Labeled a "true master of intrigue" by *Rave Reviews*, bestselling author Rebecca York continues her exciting series with #179 ONLY SKIN DEEP, coming to you next month.

When her sister is found dead, Dr. Kathryn Martin, a 43 Light Street occupant, suddenly finds herself caught up in the glamorous world of a posh Washington, D.C., beauty salon. Not even former love Mac McQuade can believe the schemes Katie uncovers.

Watch for #179 ONLY SKIN DEEP in February, and all the upcoming 43 Light Street titles for top-notch suspense and romance.

LS92

my VALENTINE 1992

Celebrate the most romantic day of the year with
MY VALENTINE 1992—a sexy new collection of four
romantic stories written by our famous Temptation
authors:

> GINA WILKINS
> KRISTINE ROLOFSON
> JOANN ROSS
> VICKI LEWIS THOMPSON

My Valentine 1992—an exquisite escape into a romantic
and sensuous world.

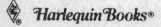 **Harlequin Books®**

VAL-92-R